Arn Hendricks and Luke Malette
were partners. They came West
together, homesteaded together.
But when a tough Texas trail boss
drove his herd across their claim,
Hendricks wanted law and Malette
wanted killing.

THE LAWBRINGERS

a big novel about the lawless West,
the way it really was, and two men who
fought side by side, and then were driven
to fight each other. . . .

THE LAWBRINGERS

by William Porter

WILDSIDE PRESS

THE LAWBRINGERS

For

My Father and Mother

THE WEST-CENTRAL FLATLAND OF KANSAS OFTEN HAS BEEN likened to a sea, and the comparison is a good one. The wind blows always, and it gives a motion like that of waves to the foreground, the things that lie close to the eyes, while the horizon at the limit of sight is always flat and dead and calm. This look has been the same as long as anybody can remember; only one ingredient has changed. Today the stuff that leans with the wind is winter wheat. Seventy-five years ago it was prairie grass, bluestem high as a man's waist sometimes, and thick as hairs on the head.

Occasionally the flatness of this land is broken by a rise, a ridge that seems to be a bud of a hill that never blossomed. These ridges are never very high, but so flat is the land that an elevation of a hundred feet can increase the reach of a man's eyes by what seems to be miles.

From one of these ridges the three men looked down at the fluid, red-yellow mass of a Texas trail herd, maybe ten thousand head, that was bedding down for the night. At one edge of these acres of longhorns five wagons sat, arranged in a rough triangle. Fires had been lighted, and there were thin stains of smoke against the furnace red of the disappearing sun.

"I think I'd better do the talking."

"Why you?"

"Because I can keep my temper, and it's hard for anybody to get rough with a man who keeps his temper."

There were three men on the ridge, but only two horses, and this exchange took place between the pair that rode double. They straddled a heavy-footed work horse with a blanket across its back. The one who wanted to do the talking sat behind, his legs uncomfortably spread by the horse's heavy rump. He was bareheaded, and the sun had burnt his hair to the color of straw where it met his forehead. The evening was hot, but since this was in the nature of a business call, he wore a black alpaca coat and a string necktie. His name was Arn Hendricks.

The man who sat in front of him wore two items of clothing that were so fine, and so obviously new, that they almost might have been considered elegant—a flat-topped brown

1

hat with a curving brim and good boots, stitched with an involved design and highly shined. The clothing in between was nondescript, old, and not very clean. He had a rifle across his lap, the familiar long-barreled Springfield that had been the standard equipment of the Union infantryman.

"That's the trouble, Arn," he muttered. "You won't lose your temper, and you'll talk—and talk and talk. Those bull-headed Texas men listen to another kind of language."

Arn glanced at the other member of the threesome.

"Maybe you'd like to handle it, Mr. Dade."

Dade was a heavy-set, bearded man who sat astride a handsome sorrel mare. He shook his head.

"You boys go ahead," he said. "I just come along to back you up."

Arn reached around the waist of his partner and, catching the barrel of the Springfield, pulled it clear.

"Sorry, Luke," he said. "But I'd feel better if the neighbor, here, carried this."

He leaned over and handed it to the man on the sorrel.

"Dade doesn't know how to handle a gun," Luke said angrily. "Listen, Arn—"

"Easy, friend," Arn said, and slapped his shoulder affectionately. "That's exactly why I gave it to him."

He thumped his heels into the sides of the plug and they moved down the slope, onto the flat stomach of the grassy sea.

The boss of the trail herd was a lean, longheaded man with a lot of jawbone. He was sitting on the tail gate of one of the wagons with a tin plate in his hand. His spoon was resting in a mound of beans, and he was eating strips of boiled salt beef with his fingers. He watched them dismount, but when they moved toward him he gave his attention back to the food. The nose of a double-barrel shotgun looked over the tail gate.

"My name is Arnold Hendricks," Arn said. "This is my partner, Luke. And this is our neighbor, Mr. Dade."

"And what's the name of your race horse?" said the Texan, glancing at the plug. "My name's McCloy. You boys grangers?"

"We're cropping a few acres," Arn said. "That's what we come to talk about. You the owner?"

"I'm the trail boss," McCloy said sharply.

"We just wanted to make sure that we were talking to the top man," Dade put in.

"You're talking to him. Go ahead."

2

From the corner of his eye Arn saw Luke stir restlessly.

"These strips we homestead are along the Dead Indian River. At least they call it a river in Kansas. Back in Ohio we'd call it a creek. Anyhow, we got crops in there, along the bottom. We know you'll have to water this herd tomorrow, and we wanted to talk to you about the route."

"The route is that way," McCloy said, pointing his finger the way he'd point a gun. "Right towards town and that railroad."

There was a moment's silence.

"You're going to have to go around," Dade said quietly. "That's where our land is—between here and Railhead. We got sorghum in, and there's pretty good corn on both places."

"You know what these herds can do when they get to moving," Arn said. "Last summer two families up the river had their soddies knocked down and the places overrun so they had to move out and start all over."

"Not to mention," Luke put in, "a couple of stolen horses and some women scared half to death."

McCloy's big jaws worked hard at the beef; he said nothing.

"You can cut off to the west here," Arn said, "until you get to the branch and then cross. River's shallow there, good bottom, good grass. And you won't be hurting anybody; that's not a claim around there. Four miles out of your way, at the most."

"Farmer boy," McCloy said, "do you know how long it takes to take ten thousand head of cattle four mile? You know what it takes out of them in this kinda heat, how much weight they'll drop?"

"That mean you're coming right through?"

"That's what it means."

In the silence that followed, Arn saw his partner's lips spread in a smile.

"Then figure on a fight," Luke said.

The Texan reached around and, without speaking, laid the shotgun across his lap. It was a wicked-looking weapon; the barrel had been shortened, and there was a leather loop anchored to the butt, so that it could be carried hung around the shoulder.

"There's not going to be any fight," Arn said sharply. "That wouldn't be smart for anybody."

"Not for sodbusters, anyhow," McCloy grunted.

"But I wouldn't want you to get me wrong," Arn said. "The only fight will be in court. If there's any damage to our places, we'll get a lawyer and slap an attachment on this herd. You won't take a nickel out of Railhead until you settle up."

3

"That scares me," McCloy said through a mouthful of beef. "I'm almost as scared of lawyers as I am of sodbusters on plow horses."

With an abrupt motion he banged the plate down and took the shotgun in both hands.

"Now whyn't you boys just get the hell out of here?" he said.

Arn turned to the other two. Dade's hands moved nervously, making fists and then opening them. The tuft of his beard quivered. He was obviously frightened.

"Come on," Arn said, laying his arm across Luke's body and pushing gently. "You heard him; he doesn't like to talk. We'll wait till we get him some place where he has to."

They walked through the yellow splash of the firelight and crawled onto the horses, while the circle of cowhands sat on their heels and watched. McCloy moved up behind them.

"You know," he said to Dade, "that's a pretty sorrel. That looks like a real blooded horse."

He scratched the edge of his jaw with a knuckle.

"You know," he said, "that's something I always wanted and never had. A pretty blooded horse."

LUKE MALETTE HAD BEEN A LITTLE TOO YOUNG TO SHOULDER a gun in the War of the Rebellion, but he had gone with the troops. He'd had to run away from home to do it, in the company of a narrow-eyed man with fancy clothes who had returned to Ohio to show the townspeople that he had already made half a fortune out of the war and was returning to make the other half. George Harkness was a renegade Englishman who had a string of sutler's wagons, rolling notion counters that sold personal items to the troops—everything from whiskey to needles and thread. Luke had stayed in the sutler business only a few months; there was money in it, all right, but money wasn't what Luke was looking for. By the winter of 1865, when he was fifteen, he had attached himself to a Pennsylvania regiment in the line before Petersburg. When the weather broke and the last push on Richmond finally came, Luke carried the traps and wore the ill-fitting uniform of a drummer boy who had died of pneumonia. There was a thing he knew he would never forget; the sound of the heavy guns in the springtime, the muttered music of the ring of iron instruments pouring fire on Richmond.

That's what woke him now; the sound of artillery, a long way off. His head snapped up; he scrambled to his knees. The first makings of daylight were visible as a blue-white line beneath the door.

4

But this wasn't Petersburg, and he wasn't fifteen any more. This was Kansas.

"Arn!" he said, nudging his bare toe into the blanket-covered figure on the straw tick beside him. "They're moving!"

They slept on the floor, although there was a bed in the house. It sat in an alcove at the back of the house. The alcove had been built on during the past two weeks; it was built of lumber, like any house in Ohio, with joists and siding and even nails. This had turned a one-room sod house into a two-room hybrid. There was a pull curtain in front of the alcove, so that it could be closed off. And inside was the bed, unslept in, brand new. The bed was a very special thing, and its purchase had taken the last nickel Luke could scrape up —which included everything Arn had to lend him.

They both slept half-dressed, and by the time Luke struggled into his fancy boots Arn was already at the door. Silhouetted in the half-light was a man on horseback. He had a shotgun across his saddle horn, and it was pointed casually in their direction.

"Came up to do you a favor," McCloy said. "Wouldn't trust anybody else to do it; came myself. Just to make sure nobody got tromped on."

"You got an early start," Luke said.

"My boys are figuring on spending tonight in town. It's a long, long push from Texas."

There was a perceptible quiver of the ground beneath their feet now.

"If that herd gets into that claim strip down there," Arn said slowly and carefully, "you're in for trouble. You can count on it."

"They're coming right through," McCloy said, swinging his hand in an arc. "You can count on that, plowboy."

"What's the matter with this country out here, anyhow?" Arn shook his head. "Look, McCloy, right now I'm a farmer. With a couple decent years I hope to get enough capital so I can buy myself a little business. All I'm trying to do is make a living. You're a cowman, but at the bottom you're just trying to do the same. What have we got to fight about? Why does everybody in the state of Kansas speak his love for his fellow men by lugging a gun?"

"I am a Texas man," McCloy said sharply. "Maybe the state of Kansas wouldn't even be here if it wasn't for the beef we push up here. I told you last night. You happen to be in the way." His mouth tightened and his eyes narrowed. "I don't like this country, and I don't like the people in it."

Luke hardly listened to the debating. The skyline at the

south was moving. They were still so far away that it was impossible to pick out anything, to say that is a longhorn, that's a man on horseback. But the motion was there.

"You go back and get them turned," Luke said through set teeth. "Turn them west."

McCloy stroked the barrel of the shotgun with his finger tips.

"You go back and crawl into bed, sonny," he said. "You look sleepy."

Luke spun on his heel and strode toward the house, over the sunburnt ground that trembled delicately under his feet. Arn came behind him, but neither of them spoke. Not until they got inside. Not until Luke had taken the Springfield from under the new bed and pulled the ramrod out and got ready to go to work. Then he broke the silence himself.

"That was pretty smart last night, giving Dade the gun. That fool out there doesn't even realize we've got one in the house."

"What do you think you're going to do with it?"

Alongside one edge of the doorframe there was a crack maybe two inches wide, as yet unrepaired from the splitting and shrinking of the summer sun. Through it the rider was clearly visible.

"I'm going to knock him off that horse, chappie," Luke said. "Right through his giz—Arn, that's Dade's horse!"

Arn bent his eye to the crack.

"Well, the man said he always wanted a real blooded horse," he said dryly. "I suppose it'll turn out that Dade always wanted a cow pony, so they traded. Or maybe Dade just wanted to stay in one piece."

Luke slid back the hammer on the Springfield; it had seen good care, and the action was good. He slid the butt to his shoulder. Then, abruptly, an arm shot across his field of vision and blocked out the target. Arn pressed the gun barrel down.

"Not on your life," he snapped. "There's maybe fifteen men in that crew, and if anything happened to McCloy, they'd take this place apart."

"Those longhorns are going to take it apart anyhow," Luke said hoarsely.

There was a look on Arn's face which Luke had seen many times before, a look of stubborn patience, a Dutch-uncle look.

"Luke," he said slowly, "give me that rifle."

Luke turned on him savagely.

"This is Kansas," he said. "This is different country, don't you know that? Back home it was good old Arn, taking care of the harum-scarum. Arn was the one that could talk, that

6

could get a job and hold it; Arn knew the nice girls and saw that Luke met them—you even introduced me to the girl that's coming out here to marry me. Arn was the one that read the papers and said that the place for a young man was West."

Nothing happened to the look, except that maybe it settled in a little deeper.

"But we're here now, and it's different." Luke was almost shouting. "Out here it takes a different kind of man—my kind. And you might as well stop telling me things, because I'm through listening!"

The muttering in the earth became a rumble as the long-horns, approaching the creek, moved faster. When Luke tried to lift the Springfield again Arn grabbed it with both hands. They wrestled fiercely for a moment, and then Arn, who carried a little more weight, twisted it free.

He hesitated and glanced around, as if looking for a place to put it, and in that instant Luke hit him. He hit him with a right hand that came all the way from his heels and landed on the underside of the jaw. The gun dropped. Arn rocked backward a couple of steps and then sat down on the dirt floor. There was a look of complete bewilderment on his face, something that Luke had never seen there before in all the years they'd known each other.

Bewildered or not, Arn got up fast and came boring in, his head down, his arms flailing wildly. Luke took a half step to the left and brought up the uppercut. His partner straightened, and Luke hit him twice, once with either hand.

Arn went down and stayed down.

And then the cold world of movement and passion snapped, and Luke looked at the man on the floor as if he had just recognized an old friend after a nightmare spent with a stranger. He dropped beside him, clutching at his shoulders.

"I'm sorry," he said. "Lordamighty, Arn, what happened? I'm sorry."

Arn propped himself on an elbow, shaking his head. The walls of the house were vibrating now, and the racket had become a low-pitched roar, with the thin yipping of the cowhands almost lost in it.

"I guess they moved even faster than we figured," he said.

Luke leaned to the crack by the doorframe again. The lead cattle were already plowing into the stream, a tangle of muscles and lather and shining horns and unnumbered hooves. Hooves that were threshing the small stand of wheat before it came to a full head, and pressing the sorghum from the unripe cane into the hard Kansas earth.

7

RAILHEAD, LIKE ABILENE AND ELLSWORTH AND LATER DODGE City, was born of an economic and geographical coincidence. Texas cattle, draining north to feed the country, met the railroad at the closest possible place, and as the iron ribbons stretched southwest across the flatlands, each of these towns, one at a time, burst into a frantic prosperity as a shipping point.

During the winter Railhead had lain idle, a town gnawed by the frosted wind, with barely enough movement to keep its veins open. Now it was June, and the town was frantically alive; before the frost came again, millions of pounds of beef would move through the pens. At one time the previous summer an incredible quarter-million head of longhorns had bedded on the plains around Railhead, waiting for the cars of the Kansas Pacific.

Railhead was a town built of anything a man could lay his hands on. Its one church, its bank, some of its houses were made of the orange-yellow limestone that underlaid the plains. But Railhead was also built of lumber hauled from Kansas City, of sod cut from the face of the earth itself, of canvas and tin and chicken wire from God knows where. Railhead had a main street forty feet wide, parallel to the railroad tracks, and this two-bladed knife cut it right down the middle; on the north side, the church and the bank and most of the merchandisers; on the other side, the rest of what it took to make up a cow town, the part of the town that people called Joyville.

In June Railhead turned its stomach up and baked in the sun, so alive that it seemed to add a heat of its own to the heat from the heavens.

Arn and Luke came into town in the middle of the morning, riding tandem on the plug. This was the day after McCloy ran his longhorns through the homestead; he had been true to his word, such as it was. The house was still standing, but there was nothing else.

The partners were in town to do business with the law, and, despite the heat, they dressed for it. Arn wore not only a clean shirt and the black alpaca coat, but also the grey pearl-button vest that had been at the bottom of a drawer since their arrival. They came without a gun. Arn had been prepared for an argument on it, but Luke had very little to say about anything today, and there was a hint of both sulkiness and apology in his silence.

"The man we want," Arn said, as he dropped the reins over the rail in front of the bank, "is this Mr. Columbine. Edward J. Upstairs, I guess." The bank was one of the few two-story buildings in town, and there was a painted hand that marked the way to Mr. Columbine.

They found him in an enormous room that took up the front half of the top floor. There was a desk big enough to sleep on, dark wood with carved legs and a top that looked like marble, and on top of it there was a heavy inkpot and a humidor for cigars, both figured in curlicues of gold.

The man who sat behind the desk had a thin cheroot deep in his mouth, as if he had half-swallowed it. He was not a tidy man; his shirt was soaked with sweat; his collar button was undone, and the necktie was coiled limply on the glass in front of him. His grey hair bushed out over his eyes. In his right hand he swung in a slow, rhythmical arc a palm-leaf fan.

"I hear you're the best lawyer in town," Arn said.

"You heard it right," said Mr. Columbine.

Arn introduced Luke first, then himself.

"I don't know much about the law," he said, "but I think we've got a case. We want to attach a man's property—or the money he got for it, if he's already been paid—for damages."

Mr. Columbine took the cheroot out of his mouth.

"There's a chair over there and another one over there," he said. "Help yourself."

They brought up the chairs and Arn told him about it. The lawyer listened with steadily slackening interest; before the story was over, he had yawned once and his eyes had been on the ceiling a half-dozen times.

"I know this McCloy. I handled the transaction this morning myself, matter of fact." He gestured modestly. "I dabble in a lot of things around here. He's been paid his share in cash, and the draft for the rest of it's on the way to Texas."

"His share?"

"Sometimes it's arranged so the trail boss gets a cut of the purchase price. He got above four thousand dollars."

"Maybe we can arrange a straight settlement and not go into court at all," Arn said. "It makes no difference, but we've got to have it. Luke, here, has got a bride-to-be coming in tomorrow night—"

"Congratulations," Mr. Columbine put in, and waved his cigar.

"—and I got plans of my own. That wasn't just a hayfield they beat down; that was our cash crop, our future. We haven't got a nickel." He grinned. "Maybe I should have mentioned that before we started talking at all."

"No difference," Mr. Columbine said, with a shrug. "Because it won't do you any good to go to law, anyhow." He leaned forward and started tracing things on the desktop with a long finger. "Look, even if I got a writ I couldn't get authority to have him arrested, and he'll be gone to Texas long before they got around to trial. But even if I got him put in jail,

9

he wouldn't stay there. How many panhandle wild men has he got in that crew? A dozen, fifteen? They'd have him out in an hour."

Hard brackets suddenly appeared around the corner of his mouth.

"If you know how weak the long arm of the law is around here," he said, "you know what I mean. If you don't, God bless your happy state of ignorance."

Arn kicked back his chair and got up.

"There must be another lawyer in town somewhere," he said.

"I'll give you one piece of advice about your money," Mr. Columbine said, completely unruffled. "Free legal advice."

"Such as?"

"Mr. McCloy is spending his riotous hitch in Railhead in a sleeping room in the Cattleman's Rest. If you want your money," he said, with a delicate wave of the cigar, "go get it."

"You mean—"

"I mean go *get* it."

"We don't do things that way," Arn said stiffly.

"*You* don't do things that way," Luke corrected him. He was out of the chair now, moving restlessly around the room, smoothing his curling black hair with the palm of his hand. He stopped by the window for a moment, looking down. Then he turned toward the door.

"I'll be back," he said to Arn. "You can wait here."

The door banged, and they heard the rattle of his boot heels on the stairway.

"Apparently a division of opinion among the plaintiffs," Mr. Columbine said, lifting an eyebrow.

"Is McCloy out there?"

The lawyer swung in his swivel, and the fan missed a couple of beats.

"Just coming across the street," he said. "Mr. McCloy has invested in some new clothes. Quite handsome."

"You and your advice," Arn said angrily, moving fast.

The world felt as if somebody had left the oven door open when he stepped from the shade of the stair well into the street; the sweat popped on his forehead. Both McCloy and Luke had moved into the line of shade cast by the building, and then walked slowly toward each other.

"Well," McCloy said. "The plowboys."

"I'd like to talk to you," Luke said.

"If you're looking for trouble, get a gun. There's sort of a rule about unarmed men."

"Where would I get a gun?" Luke asked softly, still moving, walking almost on his toes. "I'd have to buy one, and where would I get money?"

10

"Luke!" Arn said sharply, moving up behind him.

McCloy had stopped; he stood stiffly, his right hand held waist high, his fingers spread above the butt of his gun.

"Unless I got it from you," Luke said. He was still closing in. "Unless you cough up what you owe us."

"If you think I won't pull," McCloy rasped, "you're crazy—"

He tried it. As a matter of fact, he got it clear of the holster, but the barrel never came up. The polished toe of Luke's boot smashed into his wrist, and the .44 clattered against the planks of the walk. Both of them dived for it, but Malette reached it first. McCloy landed on top of him and they rolled off the edge of the walk, into the dusty gutter of the street.

The art of using side arms at close range almost could be considered a western specialty, but the art of the fist and the elbow, the thumb and the knee, was as familiar in Ohio as anywhere, and Luke's schooling had been good. He did not stay on the bottom long; McCloy pitched backward with a grunt, and Luke threw him off the way a bronc throws a rider. A moment later Arn saw a flash of metal in the sunlight as his partner's hand arced upward. It came down hard, and the barrel of the gun smacked against the Texan's skull above the ear. McCloy went limp.

Panting, Luke stood up.

"He'll sleep for a while," he said, grinning crookedly. "Well, he looked tired anyhow."

He bent over and loosened the trail boss's shirt, reached inside with both hands, and tore loose the leather money belt that was tied around his naked stomach.

"How much would you say he owed us?" he asked Arn.

"I—I don't know," Arn said. "I guess four hundred dollars would cover it."

"Better make it five," said a voice that apparently came from the heavens. "Looks like we might have a drought this summer, and that means you would have got a good price in the fall."

Mr. Edward Columbine was sitting astride the sill of his office window, like a boy on a hobbyhorse. There was a blue-barreled gun in one hand; in the other he held the holster with the belt wrapped around it.

"I took the liberty of covering you," he said, gesturing with the gun, "so I could even up the competition, if necessary. It wasn't necessary. You," he said to Luke, cocking his head, "are quite a boy."

"Five hundred," said Luke, extending a fistful of yellow-back certificates.

"While you're at it," Arn said, "don't forget that so-called

11

horse trade with Dade. He left a cow pony. Figure a hundred and fifty for Dade's mare, minus twenty dollars for the cow pony. Hundred and thirty."

"Make it one fifty," said the voice from above. "Cow ponies are a drug on the market."

Luke counted out another handful and gave it to Arn. Then he slid the money belt around McCloy's middle again, tied it tight, and replaced the Texan's gun in its holster. McCloy made a mumbling indistinguishable noise.

"Did you mean that about not owning any hardware for self-defense?" Columbine said.

"We got a Springfield at home. Varmint gun, sort of."

"I had a different kind of varmint in mind, for which a Springfield is unhandy," the lawyer said. He thrust his own gun into the holster, rewrapped the belt, and leaned down. "Catch."

"What would sodbusters want with a gun like that?" Arn said.

"That fella," Columbine said, pointing to McCloy, "won't exactly forget. Besides he's got friends around town."

The gun dropped, and Luke caught it gently in his cupped hands. He turned to Arn, his mouth half-open with pleased surprise, his eyes wide.

"I don't figure it could hurt anything," he said. "A man ought to know how to use one of these things in this country. I can bring it back."

"It's yours," Columbine said.

There was a moment's silence, and then Arn, with a shrug, turned and headed toward the plug that was tied to the rail. He pulled the lines free and climbed on, and Luke vaulted up behind him.

"Thanks," Luke called. "Thanks very much."

"Thank *you*," the lawyer said. "See you later."

Mr. Edward Columbine stood at his window and watched them go. He swung the palm-leaf fan in a slow arc against the heat, and his eyes, buried deep in the folds of his lined face, held a cool scrutiny. It was like the look of a man taking inventory of goods delivered by a fortunate mistake, with the price tag blank.

"See you later," he murmured again. "You can count on it, boy."

THERE WERE TWO PHOTOGRAPHS IN THE SODDIE IN WHICH Luke and Arn Hendricks lived. They sat on top of the battered bureau, one on either side of the square mirror, and both of them belonged to Luke. One of them showed a girl with blond hair and an unmistakable grace in her body, de-

12

spite the artificial pose and the fussy dress. The other was of Luke himself, Luke ten years younger, not yet a man, dressed in the ill-fitting uniform of a Pennsylvania drummer boy; his spine starched to attention, his cap bill square and level above his dark eyes, the Springfield propped on his shoulder. The rifle was too big for him; the grim intensity of his face reflected the effort with which he held it.

He had picked up the Springfield from the battlefield at Petersburg, and carried it through the rest of the campaign. He had learned to shoot with it, and shoot well, but through an odd coincidence—or a series of coincidences—it had never been fired in earnest. Luke had been in the middle of several actions, but he had never had a chance to pull down on a Johnny Reb.

The new gun, the gift of lawyer Columbine, was a lot easier to handle than the Springfield. And Luke was learning to handle it. When he first got home with it he had cut a slit through the bottom of the holster and fitted it with a strip of buckskin, so it could be tied down to the leg. Beginning the next morning, he wore it constantly, and made practice pulls a hundred times a day.

"You're getting handy with that thing in a big hurry," Arn observed once. "Like a thirsty man is handy with a dipper."

"Wish I had a nickel for every rod I walked over battlefields, during the war, looking for a holster gun. Springfields there were plenty of, and nobody cared if you picked one up —least of all the gents they'd belonged to in the first place. But officers had the holster guns, and not many got too loose. Captain used to let me clean his Colt, and sometimes bang away at a knothole." Luke shook his head. "That captain was a man with no pride. Can you imagine a man who wouldn't even take care of his own gun? Clumsy with it, too."

"Not handy, you mean," Arn grinned.

"Me, I was handy with a gun the first time I laid hands on one."

"Maybe. But you got to admit it looks a little silly on a sodbuster. It also gets in the way of your work."

They were planting corn now, hoping against reason that the weather would be wet enough and the fall long enough for a crop to make; it was the only chance.

"Makes my right arm stronger," Luke said solemnly. "For using that hoe when the time comes to cultivate this stuff, chappie. Besides, look at the cottontails I knock over."

It took Monday afternoon and the oncoming evening to make him forget about the .38. On that day he forgot everything.

They came in from the field early, in midafternoon, and gave the house a final, painstaking picking up. They scrubbed

13

what furniture there was with soap and water; they scraped and polished the sheet iron that, placed over a waist-high limestone chimney, served as a stove; they checked the curtain that closed off the alcove to make sure it slid easily on its rope track.

"It's not going to be very private," Arn said. "You know, this hot weather and all, I think maybe I'll sleep down by the creek for a while."

"The house belongs to both of us, and it was my idea to get married, not yours." A slight touch of color showed under the skin of Luke's dark cheeks. "Of course," he mumbled, "if you think it would be cooler out there, you suit yourself."

Later, while he was shaving, he suddenly stopped and looked around the place again, as if he'd never seen it before.

"Luke's castle." He laughed dryly. "Judas Priest, how I hate to bring her into this."

"She wanted to come, didn't she?" Arn said. "You ought to know her well enough by now. She'll like it fine."

"That's not exactly what I mean. A man like me ought to be able to provide more. I—I'd look better."

"You mean that a jewel like you needs a better setting to be properly appreciated." Arn grinned.

After a long moment Luke grinned back.

"What else has a man got to give a woman but himself, as big and as fancy and as exciting as he can be? Arn, I'll bet you think the first thing a man owes his wife is a living. I think it's the last thing. The first thing he owes her is to be one hell of a ripsnorting man."

"For her sake? Or his own?"

There was a thudding of hooves in the sandy dust of the yard, the rattle of wheels. Company was rare out here. Arn saw Luke turn and glance toward the gun.

"If the Texas boys come, they won't come in a buggy," Arn said. "Take it easy."

The rig was a gaudy thing, with yellow spokes and red hubs. The chestnut gelding that pulled it was also a looker, and the Spanish harness was crested with spangles. All this elegance made the man who stepped out of it look downright shabby. Mr. Edward Columbine wore both a coat and an embroidered vest and his hair was almost combed, but he still looked like something off the bottom layer of a recently unpacked trunk.

"Well," said Mr. Columbine cheerily, as Arn ushered him in, "tonight's the night, is it not?"

He held out a fistful of cheroots, like a bouquet.

"It is," Luke said, in some astonishment. "How did you know?"

"The difference between a good lawyer and a bad one,"

Mr. Columbine said, "is that a bad one remembers what he has to, but a good one remembers everything. You mentioned shipping in a bride when you were in the office the other day. Would you consider it meddling if I asked you exactly what the plan was?"

"She gets in on the train tonight. We figured she'd stay at the preacher's tonight, and Arn and I would come back here."

"And for transportation, I suppose you plan to use the plug?"

"Sort of thought I might hire a rig tomorrow morning. For the church, and then to bring her out here." Luke shrugged and grinned wryly. "Of course, sooner or later she's got to get used to the plug."

Mr. Columbine cocked his head in the direction of the buggy outside the door.

"How'd you like to use that for the next couple, three days?"

There was a pause.

"How much?" Luke said.

"We'll call it a gesture of the romantic West to a beautiful woman."

"You mean you drove all the way out here just for that?"

"Not on your life," Columbine said. "I wanted to see this place. I don't have much contact with the sodbusters around here, but you gents don't strike me as being the type. Incidentally," he finished offhand, "that corn won't make it."

"It's a chance," Arn said. "The only one." Columbine was frankly inspecting the premises now; he stood with his hands in his pockets, the cheroot gripped tightly in his teeth, his head swinging slowly as he took it in.

"We don't plan to stay here forever," Arn said, with a trace of apology in his voice. "I'm trying to get enough capital to get set up in business in town."

"What kind of business?"

"Hardware. And what goes with it."

"What about you?" Columbine said to Luke. "Going to partner?"

"Maybe. Or stay here. I don't know. I just came West because it sounded like my kind of country."

Columbine gave him a quick look and then, with slow emphasis, nodded his head.

"You're right," he said. "The word about you handling that Texas hoot owl is already going around. Railhead's talking about you, boy. I suspect you of having a future."

Luke smoothed the tie once more and reached for his coat.

"We've got to move," he said. "It's late."

"You'd better finish dressing."

"I'm finished."

A tight grin lifted one side of the lawyer's mouth.

"Well, not exactly," he said.

With the fingers of one hand he reached out and slid the .38 across the table, his eyes level with Luke's.

"After all, you're not just a sodbuster any more. You're somebody. And after all, this is Kansas."

THE DEPOT OF THE KANSAS PACIFIC RAILROAD AT RAILHEAD was not yet finished, although it had been in full use for almost a year. It was planned for two stories; the bottom one was complete, and one end of the upper had been finished enough to support a good-sized clock, but the rest of it was bones; corner posts and stanchions sticking into the sky.

The most elegant touch was the line of tall lamps which lighted the platform, round globes on painted iron posts. As the hard-shelled June bugs gathered around the oil flames on a summer night, so the citizens of Railhead gathered around the posts to watch the train come in. Since it was a Monday night, which meant nothing special going on in town, the gathering was a little larger than usual. Arn and Luke stood in the middle of it. Mr. Columbine, after a delicate cough to indicate his discretion, had declined the invitation to come along.

When she gets off that train, Arn told himself, beating the words into his brain, she gets off as Luke's wife. All right, so they haven't said the words yet; it makes no difference, she is as good as his wife now. The competition is over. The prize has been awarded.

Actually there hadn't been much competition. Luke had hardly been aware of it. Mattie, having a full share of the delicate equipment that females use in detecting such things, certainly had been. But she had never spoken of it—quite probably because Arn had never brought the subject up in the first place. For a short time after he had introduced Luke to her, back in Ohio, there had been a casual triangle; sometimes the three of them went places together, sometimes the men took turns at squiring. Then Luke took over altogether. As far as Arn knew, there wasn't a case on record of Luke wanting a woman that he didn't get. And so he accepted it; he even did some noble, detached thinking, about how good it would be for Luke in settling him down.

But the last few months, the last few weeks, out here in this country where the kind of women you took seriously were few and far between, Arn had found Mattie Larson a lot on his mind.

16

The KP engine blinked around the curve, its whistle an irritable high scream.

"You look fine," he said to Luke, in his best buck-up voice. "Wonderful."

"That's what I figure," Luke said. His teeth flashed in the half-light from the lamps. "You're the one that's shaking, chappie."

That habit of calling people "chappie" was Luke's one inheritance from the flashy Englishman with whom he had gone off to the wars. It always needled Arn a little; there was something patronizing in it.

"Look, you meet her here and I'll see you at the rig—"

"Come here!" Luke grabbed his coattails.

She was the first one off the train. The conductor, obviously a man with an eye for a good-looking woman, held her arm a little longer than was necessary in helping her down. There were noises indicating appreciation and high esteem from the assembled gentlemen. Luke and Arn stood gawking at her, frozen where they stood, as if this moment could not possibly be true.

Finally Luke came alive and dived for her. He kissed her once, violently but briefly. Then he caught a breath and did it with more finesse and at a considerably greater length. The citizens cheered. Then he spun her toward Arn.

"Well, come on," he said. "Stop digging your toe in the ground and say hello to the lady."

Arn had a vague idea about saying hello at a distance, but she didn't see it that way. Both arms came around him. The smell of her hair was like something from a place he'd never been but always wanted to go.

"What in heaven's name," he heard her say in his ear, "is *that*, Luke?"

He let her go and stepped aside. She was looking with one cocked eyebrow at the holster thonged to Luke's hip.

"In Kansas," Luke laughed, "this is what a gentleman carries instead of a cane."

"It looks ridiculous," she said. "On some of the western wild men, maybe, but not on the man I'm marrying."

"All right," Luke said, "I promise not to wear it to the wedding. Arn, if you'll take the suitcases, I'll take the lady."

And then, with a whoop of laughter, he swung his arms beneath her, lifted her, and started for the end of the platform where the rig was hitched. Arn filled both arms with baggage and followed. They moved clear of the crowd, past the last of the tall lamps. Luke was almost to the buggy when the voice came out of the shadows.

17

"The farmer boy grew up fast. Now he's got both a woman and a gun."

Two men moved into the edge of the light. Arn knew both faces. They had been in the firelight behind the wagons of McCloy's trail herd. From the tail of his eye he saw Luke let Mattie down.

"Go ahead," Arn said sharply. "I'll take care of it."

"It'll take both of you," said one of them. "You with the gun, especially."

It would have been a hard thing to say exactly what they'd planned on doing. When the one who did the talking reached for his hip, he might have been making a threat, nothing else. Maybe he meant business. Whether or not he meant it, he got it. Luke's palm slapping the hardwood of the handle of the .38 made a clear, sharp sound.

Arn whirled and drove his arm across the girl's waist, flinging her behind him. Her heels caught in the planking of the platform. She fell backward and he threw himself beside her, both arms across her body, holding her down. There were four shots.

When he looked up, one of the Texans was already down and the other was moving backward into the darkness, firing as he went. The second of these shots hit Luke; Arn saw him twitch convulsively at the impact, but he did not go down. Somewhere behind them on the platform a woman screamed loudly, senselessly. Arn scrambled to his feet and made for Luke, who had transferred the .38 to his other hand. He fired blindly into the darkness until the hammer snapped against an empty shell.

Then he turned, the one-sided grin frozen on his face, and slid into Arn's arms, like a child who is very tired.

DOCTOR HOMER CHUBB STUCK THE SWAB INTO THE BOTTLE of brown liquid, turned it a couple of times, lifted the flap of the incision with the probe, and then struck a pose with the swab uplifted in one hand.

"What's that?" the young man muttered.

"You're gonna think it's a hot horseshoe, but it's just carbolic. Go ahead and yell. It'll do you good." He made a couple of quick digging motions with the swab, then pitched it aside and looked over the tops of his glasses in surprise. "No?"

"I'm not the kind that yells."

"Well, cheers for you, my lad," said Doctor Chubb. "I'm beginning to think you're quite a boy. Heard about the tussle at the station."

"Will he be able to walk again?"

The girl was sitting on the upholstered bench against the wall. She was holding hands with another young man, but Homer Chubb, without making any kind of real diagnosis of the situation, was pretty certain that the motive was mutual comfort rather than romance. He scowled. From the looks of them, Chubb said to himself, you'd think somebody was going to die.

"My dear girl," he snapped, "he will not only walk again, he will run like a frightened deer, if he wants to. The slug was imbedded in the thigh, the *fascia lata*. It'll be a lot less bother than a carbuncle, if there are no complications."

He turned to the pan of water that was boiling on the little coal-oil stove.

"And there'll be no complications," he went on. He gingerly splashed hot water into an empty basin, mixed it with cold, and started washing his hands.

"I never saw such a hand-washing man in my life," the girl said. "That's the tenth time at least. Why don't you just go ahead and sew it up?"

"If I supply the medical care," Doc Chubb growled, "would you be good enough to confine yourself to the usual function of female moans and vapors?"

The handle of a pair of forceps stuck over the end of the flat pan; he gingerly picked them up and dredged out a needle already threaded with gut. He waved it in the air a few times to cool it enough for handling. Then Doc Chubb got down to his sewing.

"If you haven't seen this before," he said as he worked, "it's because most physicians are fatheads who refuse to keep up with the march of science. Over in England there's a medical fella who's got a notion about pus and gangrene and all that. He thinks things should be clean. I mean, really clean, fire-clean. I think he's right."

The incision took two stitches, and he tied them off neatly and clipped them short. Then more on general principles than anything else—there were a lot of gaps in Doc Chubb's understanding of this new medicine they called antiseptic— he swabbed the whole area with carbolic again, and bandaged it.

"And now, mister," he said to Arn, "if you'll take the young lady out of here, we'll get this lad back into his pants."

While Luke dressed, the doctor rolled down his sleeves, attached his cuffs again, and slid into his claw-hammer coat. Then he paddled across the room to a clothes tree that stood in the corner, and with loving care took down the two revolvers that hung from a peg, each by its own belt.

"Those yours?" Luke said. "I've been coveting."

The Peacemakers were a matched pair with ivory handles.

19

On each of them the doctor's initials were worked into the carving, along with a design of intertwining leaves and flowers. There was a ring at the bottom of the grip, with a thin strand of buckskin tied through it; the barrel and frame had been heavily silvered, and a variation of the leaves-and-flowers design ran the length of the barrel on either side. The holsters were thin black leather, cut low enough so most of the trigger guard was exposed. Both the holsters and the belts were rather plain—the frame should not overpower the picture—and the only ornamentation was a stitching in silver beads.

"Found a Mexican who did most of the work," Chubb said proudly. "Took almost a year."

"For those," Luke said, his eyes wide and rapt, "a man could give his right arm and figure he had a bargain."

Chubb hitched the belts around his substantial stomach so that they crossed at the buckles, and then worked the holsters into position.

"What does a man like you need with those things?" Luke said. "I mean—well, you're not exactly young any more, and there's not many people around here who'd be gunning for you, what with doctors being scarce the way they are—"

"But you never can tell," Doc Chubb said ominously. Then he grinned, a little self-consciously. "Lots of people ask me that. Maybe I wear them because I can get by with it out here. Because a man is more of a man with a weapon at his side. Or maybe it's just that I think the romance is going out of the world, and I'm an old romantic." He shook his head. "Never had to fire these things yet. But if I ever do, I'll be ready."

Then a ferocious scowl came over his round, bespectacled face.

"Reach, partner!" he said fiercely, and they both pulled simultaneously and were still standing there with the guns in their hands, laughing, when l a w y e r Columbine banged through the door.

"Homer, is this lad going to be all right?" he asked anxiously.

"He's going to drop dead any minute," Doc Chubb growled. "Internal bleeding. Can't you see, you dumb fool?"

Columbine mopped his face with a white handkerchief the size of a dinner napkin.

"How's the cowhand that got plugged?"

"The slug grazed his top rib and went into the shoulder joint. He'll never be able to do much with that arm again. I patched him up first because it looked kind of bad."

"Where is he now?"

20

"How should I know? Some of his friends came around here and took him off with them."

"They try to make any more trouble?"

Luke shook his head. Columbine chewed his lip for a moment and then, with sudden violence, smacked his knotted fist into the bench.

"Those ramrods ought to be in jail!" he exploded. "I got the story from half a dozen people; they pulled first, and this lad was with his bride-to-be—Homer, did you know that the marshal stood there and watched the whole thing? Just stood and watched?"

"Didn't know it," Chubb said, "but I'm not surprised."

"He didn't even come down here and try to pick up the one that was winged. You're the mayor of this town and I'm the city attorney, and it's up to us to find another kind of man."

He looked at Luke for a long moment and then, turning, looked at Doc Chubb. Their eyes met and held. Finally the lawyer broke the silence.

"Malette," he said, mopping his face again, "do you want to plow corn the rest of your life, or would you like to talk about a real job?"

SINCE IT WAS AT THE BACK OF THE BUILDING, DOC CHUBB'S office faced, not the street, but what would have been the alley in an ordinary town. There were no alleys in Railhead, and behind the bank there was nothing but flatland. The small window in the outer office provided a view of a black horizon line against a moonless sky, and that was all.

Arn and the girl sat side by side in the two reed-bottomed chairs.

It's sure taking quite a while to get into those pants," Arn said. He had said it several times before.

"Well, you said the man who breezed in a while ago was a lawyer," Mattie pointed out. "And you know how it is with lawyers. Just listen."

The low mutter of conversation beyond the door had not let up since Columbine arrived.

"You don't suppose he's in any trouble with the law?"

"Not in this town," Arn said.

Their eyes met for a moment and then hers flicked away. He studied her face. There was a peculiar tension there; there was more than fatigue from the trip and concern for Luke. On a weaker face the look could have been a pout, but on Mattie it was something more than that.

"By the way, Arn," she said, coming out of it with a smile

21

that was a little too bright, "Lucy Dobson wanted me to give you her fondest. She misses you."

"That's funny," Arn drawled. "She didn't even seem to know I was around when I lived back there. You mean the pretty daughter of the richest man in Cincinnati started honing as soon as I left?"

"Well, all I know is that—"

"Or would you just be saying nice things to make me feel good," he went on, smiling, "knowing that I've always been backward with the ladies?"

"Arnold Hendricks, she said it!"

"Well, thank you very much, Mattie," he said gravely.

The inner door came open and Luke came out with one arm around the doctor's shoulder. Luke was not a tall man, but the balding head of Homer Chubb barely came to his chin.

"He's going to be perfectly all right, understand," Chubb said. "Only it'd go a little easier if he kept off that leg as much as he could for a couple days. He sure can't do any traipsing back to that homestead tonight; the lawyer, here, says they can find him something at the hotel."

"Don't see why he'll ever have to go back to that farm at all," Columbine grunted.

"If I never do it's too soon," Luke said. His dark eyes swung from the girl to his partner, and a foolish phrase crossed Arn's mind: Christmas tree. Like a kid under the Christmas tree. The same look had been in his eyes as he stood beneath lawyer Columbine's window, clutching the .38.

"You're through sod-busting, too, chappie," he said.

"I guess I'm lost," Arn said. "Maybe it'd be clearer if you went back a ways."

"I've got a job." He slid a finger along Mattie's cheek. "Money in the hand every month, gal. A hundred dollars. And now, if it's the same to you, you both can start acting more respectful. You're looking at the law."

"He's hired for town marshal," Columbine said.

"You've already accepted?" the girl asked quickly.

"He has." Columbine shook his head in mock amazement. "But he drives a real bargain. He wanted nothing to do with it, Hendricks, unless we also took care of you."

"I can manage," Arn said stiffly.

"Meaning," the lawyer went on, as if he hadn't heard it, "a loan to put you into the hardware business. We can work it out at the bank. How much you going to need?"

Arn felt a little dizzy, as if the ground had rocked beneath his feet. He swallowed a couple of times.

"I'd—I'd have to think about it," he said.

He had figured on five years of fighting the prairie and the

22

weather before he built up enough to start thinking about a business of his own. Five years; and now here it was, as simple as speaking a half-dozen words.

"I've got nothing for security," he said. "Except for my half of the claim out there, and maybe fifty dollars' worth of equipment, all put together."

"We'll take that," Columbine said, "and have to figure the rest of it for an act of faith. Anyhow, we'll work it out, because Luke isn't interested unless we do. And we're figuring strong on Luke."

"Why?" Mattie said, coming to her feet. "Why won't any other man do?"

"Wait a minute," Luke grinned. "Mattie, you sound like they were drafting me. I want this job."

"Madam," Doc Chubb said, pushing his slipping glasses up his nose, "the history of Kansas—the history of the whole western frontier—is built around strong peace officers. One-man law. It's the only kind of law that works out here, if you can get the right man. Look at this Earp fella, and Hickok—"

"We've never had it that way," Columbine said. "We've only had a town marshal for nineteen months and in that time we've had eleven of 'em! We've hired saddle bums out of Texas and ex-officers who'd jumped the Army and Indian scouts half-blind from the sun. Anybody who'd volunteer and seemed to know the butt from the muzzle of a gun."

Smiling wryly, Luke slid onto the chair beside her and dropped a hand on her arm.

"You still don't see this right," he said. He gave Columbine and the doctor a quick look. "Arn and my gal here can get me to the hotel," he said.

They shuffled their feet awkwardly for a moment and cleared their throats and then left. Arn started after them.

"You stick," Luke said. "This is a family talk."

"It doesn't look like there's much to talk about," Mattie said. "You've already settled it." She had been sitting rigid, her eyes on the floor, but suddenly her eyes came up and swept over his face and she leaned toward him until her forehead touched his chin. "Luke, I wish you wouldn't."

He slid his hand along her hair, the straw-colored mass of it loose and spreading at her shoulders. Arn stared with painful intensity through the window into the black emptiness of the night.

"You're afraid for me, I suppose," he heard Luke murmur. "Don't worry. I'm bullet-proof. Guarantee it."

"That's part of it, but only part." There was a rustling swish of taffeta as she moved away from him, and Arn turned back into the group again. "I don't like the way they talk about this country," she said, almost fiercely. "This is Kansas, they say, and they say it as if it excused every silliness and sinfulness and stupidity in the world. There's no apology the way they say it; they wag their heads and look solemn and talk about needing one-man law, but they like it that way."

"This is a different kind of country," Luke said.

"Maybe. But people are people, aren't they? Luke, I came out here to work my fingers raw for you. I knew it would be rough and wild and that we'd have to fight until we dropped. But it's different. There's something else; you pull it in when you breathe. Arn—you know what I mean, don't you?"

Luke's dark eyes, points of black in the shadow of the thin brows, swung toward him. And one corner of his mouth lifted, waiting for the answer.

"I know we better get this boy to bed," Arn said. "Otherwise he's going to make a sorry-looking bridegroom in the morning."

"You mean you still figure on the ceremony tomorrow?" Mattie said. "Well, gentlemen—I wouldn't want to seem backward, but it's my wedding, and if it's all the same to everybody, I'd rather have the groom all in one piece."

She said it lightly, but there was nothing light about the silence that settled in the room. Arn saw his partner's eyes widen with astonishment, and then hard brackets settled around the corners of his mouth.

"Like you say, lady, you're the bride."

"I'm pretty tired from the trip, and maybe shaken up by this business tonight. Let's just don't worry about it for a couple of days. Then when things get settled, we'll talk about it."

The silence again, tight and painful; Arn had a feeling that they stood with their hands braced against a wall to keep it from caving in.

"Why not?" Luke shrugged. The gesture was a little too broad. "I guess we're all shaken up tonight. Now I'd appreciate it if you'd get me over to that hotel. I got a honing for a feather bed."

IT HAD BEEN ARRANGED FOR MATTIE TO SPEND THE NIGHT IN the home of the Reverend Minner, of Methodist persuasion and Railhead's only man of the cloth. The Reverend and his wife had a regular traffic of respectable and unattached young ladies through the parsonage; there was almost no other place in town for them to go. The Reverend's house, built of limestone block and painted white, was next to the church.

After he'd seen Luke to bed, Arn walked the girl the two

blocks. It was after midnight, and there was a fingernail of moon, red as the heart of a campfire climbing the outer edges of the sky.

They said very little until they were almost to the house. Then, abruptly, Arn threw it at her:

"You weren't honest tonight."

"What about?"

"The wedding."

"Arn, don't plague me with trying to talk seriously. I said I was upset; I am."

"But you weren't honest—that business about wanting a whole bridegroom. There's a lot more to it than that and Luke knows it."

"Arn, don't—"

Then she stopped, pulled in a deep breath, and faced him.

"All right," she said. "I suppose it sounds silly, but if I'd found him with a broken leg from—from some horse kicking him, things would have been different. If he'd been so sick from the fever that he couldn't get out of bed, I'd have married him in the bedroom tomorrow morning. But tonight—"

"It's not as if he'd gone out and deliberately got himself mixed up in a shooting scrape. He was defending himself, all of us," Arn said, and as he said it he realized he was trying to convince not only Mattie but himself. "When you backed out tonight it hurt him. Didn't you see his face? His pride's never been hurt like that before."

"His pride? Are we to be married for the sake of his pride?"

It was as if she'd heard the words spoken that afternoon in the sod house on the prairie and now gave them back.

"That's not what I meant—" He reached out suddenly and grabbed her by the shoulders, moved his face close to hers. "If you came here to marry him, get it done!" he said hoarsely. "For God's sake, do it as quick as you can, or I—"

The words jammed in his throat, and nothing more came out.

"What difference does it make to you, Arn?"

"None." He let her go and stepped back. "No difference in the world. Good night, Mattie."

As he turned, a sharp explosion cut the night, and then another. Up the street somebody whooped a wild *yee-hoooo!*

"Welcome to Kansas," Arn said and quickly walked away.

ON A HOT FRIDAY AFTERNOON, FOUR DAYS AFTER HE HAD AS-sumed the office of town marshal for the city of Railhead, Luke Malette for the first time shot and killed a man. It was strictly in the line of duty. The man, Hamilton Otter, was a part-Cherokee buffalo hunter who had worked off and on for the Kansas Pacific and had recently been discharged for stealing hides. On the day of his unhappy end he had rented a saddle horse from Patterson's livery for a couple of hours; when he'd returned it, he had engaged in a furious quarrel with Ernest Patterson, the owner, over some deep lashes which indicated the animal had been quirted severely. During this quarrel Otter, who was armed, had forced Mr. Patterson at gun point to accompany him to the loft in which the stable's feed was stored, whereupon Otter had laced the proprietor's feet together with his belt and then attempted to set fire to the loft. Fortunately an employee had succeeded in summoning the marshal who, arriving at the stable, had caught Otter in the yard just as he was mounting another animal. Otter had fired first and the marshal had promptly felled him with two shots, the first through the left shoulder and the second through the throat.

The marshal had then taken Otter to the office of Dr. Homer Chubb for treatment, but the man was dead on arrival. Acting in his capacity of coroner, Dr. Chubb had announced that Otter had died as a result of gunshot wounds inflicted by an officer of the law in the performance of his duty and that no inquest was necessary.

Fortunately the fire in the loft was extinguished without particular damage.

Arn was in Kansas City when this happened, ordering and arranging for the delivery of the stock of goods for his new store. He heard about it immediately upon his return, of course. Luke himself had almost nothing to say about it.

"This chappie wanted shooting, that's all," he said, his dark eyes fixed on the empty air, one corner of his mouth lifted slightly. "I obliged."

It was from the Major that Arn got the most complete— and objective — version. Major Elihu Watson had a store building and some furnishings for sale, and Columbine had suggested that Arn approach him.

"Don't give him much. He'll have to take what he can get. The Major is in a bad way." There had been contempt in the lawyer's eyes. "Very, very bad, financially."

"What's the trouble?"

"Just start him talking about himself, and he'll tell you everything. Fermented spirits are great for loosening the tongue, and the Major is generally fermented to the ears." He shook his head. "He's on the city council, by the way. Dreadful. Gives the administration a bad name."

So on the morning after Arn's return from Kansas City, the Major showed him around the store. The place was one room, limestone on three sides, frame on the other. The furnishings were sparse, to say the least: two counters, an oddly assorted group of sagging shelves, and two oil lamps suspended from the unfinished ceiling.

"I was in the grocery business, you understand. Hah!" He snorted through the straggling yellow of his mustache. "I presume I decided on the grocery trade because of my long experience at mismanagement of Army commissaries."

Arn estimated that today the Major was fermented, if not to the ears, at least to the shoulder blades. There was a hitch in his walk, and his eye wandered. He wore a coat and trousers that had never been introduced to each other, and anchored to the belt which circled his soft waist was a holster which held an old Army revolver.

"When were you retired from the Army?" Arn asked, for the sake of something to say.

"I was cashiered five years ago," the Major said promptly. "Do I look old enough for retirement? I know—I look as old as these damn prairies. An optical illusion. My boy, you see the dissipated shell of what was once a man."

He laughed, a sharp, braying sound.

"Of course, I did not inform these yokels that I left the Army by request when I came here. Instead I spread a discreet rumor that I had been so shot up by the Rebels that the trooper's life was impossible. For a couple of years it worked fine." He tapped his breastbone with a long finger. "Sir, you look at a man who is a councilman of the city government."

"I heard that—"

"Nobody's thought to kick me out yet. Which shows you how important the city council is in Railhead." He tidied the mustache with his thumb and forefinger. "I'm a Massachusetts man, my boy. Don't confuse me with these ignorant Kansans."

He sat down heavily on the counter, and looked around the room as if he had never seen it before, as if he were alone in a strange place.

"Have you set a price yet?" Arn asked uncomfortably.

"Later," the Major said. "We will talk business at the last possible moment. I detest business." His eyes came into focus and moved toward Arn. "Columbine's new marshal, this Malette fellow, is a friend of yours?"

Arn nodded.

"Did you hear about yesterday's skirmish?"

"Several stories. All incomplete, most of them different."

"I helped quench the flames in the stable personally. I will tell you the story."

And he told it. With alcoholic vigor and enthusiasm, and in considerable detail, with many gestures and a great range of inflections.

"He's going to make a great marshal for Columbine," he said finally. "There was that thing in his eyes. When it was over—you know what I mean? As if he'd had a couple of drinks: the flame in his eyes, the exhilaration — Do you drink?"

"Sociably."

"For an upcoming merchant prince, that's plenty. At any rate, you understand the metaphor. With the gun still in his hand and his eyes half-closed, as if he'd had a couple of drinks."

The Major wiped his mouth with the back of his hand.

"He'll make a great killer," he said casually. "All for the sweet sake of the law, of course."

Arn pulled in his breath sharply. There was a tight silence. Then Watson, with an amazingly fast motion, whipped the ancient Army revolver from his belt and pointed it at an invisible something on the wall.

"Bang," he said. "Bang, bang." He brayed with laughter.

"What did you mean about Luke being Columbine's marshal? Maybe the lawyer's the city attorney, but Luke was appointed for the town."

"Columbine's tame marshal," the Major said loudly.

Arn reached out a hand and sank his fingers into Watson's filthy shirt, just beneath the throat. He twisted hard.

"Luke won't be a hired gunhand for anybody," he said. "He won't do anybody's dirty laundry or step outside the law. Get it straight."

"He will not be required to step outside the law. He'll keep the peace, which is what they want. Let go, boy; that hurts a little."

Arn let his hand slide away. The Major's eyes wandered again, this time to the window that opened onto the wide street. A woman in a yellow sunbonnet passed, lecturing the tow-haired eight-year-old who trailed her.

"I had hopes for this town," the Major said dreamily. "I came here before they started bringing cattle. It was in May —a wet May that year—and the prairie grass was as high as your belt. Just a few buildings then. Yellow limestone. A small world of green grass and butter-colored buildings. Sometimes I still . . ."

The words trickled off, and the eyes wandered back to Arn.

"You know, if I ever sober up, I might do this town a lot

of good yet. With help, of course. You and me. A great combination of levelheaded men."

Arn met his eyes for a moment and then, turning, moved slowly down the counter in the other direction. His hand slid along the smooth wood and, when he lifted it, the fingers were red with dust.

"I expect," the Major said, very quietly, "that you are impatient to talk business."

Arn got the place, lock, stock and barrel, for eighteen hundred dollars. A ridiculous price—but, after all, as the Major himself pointed out, eighteen hundred dollars will buy a great deal of whiskey at a dollar a quart.

WHEN MATILDA LARSON LEFT OHIO AND CAME TO KANSAS SHE left one world and entered a new one as irretrievably as if she had crossed an ocean. There had been little family to leave behind her; an older sister and her husband with whom she'd lived for the past two years, a grim and money-tight situation complicated by her brother-in-law's habit of using Mattie's virtues as a pin to prick his rather slovenly wife. When Mattie climbed on the train in Cincinnati, all of them knew that the farewells were final. Nothing was said, but nothing needed saying. She would not be back.

Thus when Mattie decided—or rather, when she heeded an inner voice that was too persistent to ignore—that she needed a longer look before the wedding leap, she had no place to go. She knew two towns, and she was in the second one with all her possessions and seven dollars in her pocketbook. Here she had to stay.

Luke knew this, of course. Mattie thought that perhaps this accounted for his easy acceptance of her decision, and in a perverse way it rankled her a little. If the man thought he could lie beneath the tree with his hands up and wait for the plum to drop because sooner or later gravity conquers all, he had another think coming.

But this was not all of it, not the only reason that Luke did not press her and act the distraught suitor in her first days in Railhead. Luke had other things in his head; somewhere a new fire had been lighted, and sometimes it was almost as if he had something else to love.

That thought always shook her, registered not so much in her mind as in her stomach. Yet this new Luke had attractions that pulled hard on her. The work on the farm had done wonderful things for him; she had never seen him look so well. And with money—he'd said something about lawyer Columbine advancing some wages—he was wearing the kind of clothes he wanted to wear. A dark broadcloth suit, a fine lawn shirt, a felt hat with a curling brim. And opal cuff links. The cuff links had been her father's and she had given them to Luke before he came West.

"Finally," he'd said, when she first saw him in his new finery, "I've got something to wear them in."

On Tuesday morning, some two weeks after her arrival in Railhead, Mattie went to see Doctor Homer Chubb about a job. She found him behind the littered table he called his desk, coat off and cuffs detached, his nose buried in a booklet—literally buried, because the Doc was nearsighted, in spite of his glasses.

"New copy of the *Lancet*," he grunted, waving the book at her. "British medical publication. Difficult enough to find one in New York, say nothing about getting one out here." He tossed it on the desk. "Nine dollars it cost me, when you figure everything. Worth it, though."

"More about this Englishman and his clean medicine?"

"Lister." Doc Chubb nodded. "Antisepsis."

"I was watching you the other day when you fixed up Luke. This new way complicates things, doesn't it? No more giving a scalpel a couple of licks across your boot and then cutting away. Doctor, you need help." She smiled brightly. "Because of difficult financial circumstances, I am available for seven dollars a week."

"Hah! Florence Nightingale, Clara Barton—eh?"

"What's so funny about it? I worked some with a doctor back home, a very good man; if you'd like to write for a refer—"

"I don't care who you worked with; so far as I'm concerned, you'd have to be educated all over again."

"If we start the education right now," Mattie said, "it'll be finished that much sooner. . . . Six dollars a week?"

"Nobody pays me; I won't be able to pay you anyhow," Doc Chubb grumbled. "Hell, I might as well owe you seven dollars a week as six."

His wide, almost babyish, blue eyes sought hers and held them for a moment. He spoke quietly.

"What about marrying the marshal? Will he like it if—"

"That's hanging fire for a little while," she said quickly. She'd known that one was coming, and she had practiced the answer to herself. "Until I get squared away out here in this new country."

Doc Chubb thoughtfully stroked his bare head with a chubby hand.

"Hope you're thinking things out," he said. "That boy could use the right kind of woman. After all, you did come out here to marry him—gives you a certain amount of responsibility—"

"I've heard about my responsibility to Luke before!" she said sharply. "More than enough. Can you use help, or can't you?"

"Flinty type, huh? All right, excuse me." He rocked back in the chair and with frank and unscientific enthusiasm inspected her from her ankles up. "If you're going to be around this office, I'm going to start wishing I was twenty years younger."

He sighed heavily.

"We will start the education with a little of the theory behind the practice. Take off your bonnet and prepare to hear about the germ."

WORKING ALONE AT THE BUSINESS OF SETTING UP STOCK, UN-crating and lifting and shoving and shelving, was hard on a man with only two arms. But paying for help would be even harder on a man whose every breath was drawn in on credit. Arn worked sixteen, sometimes eighteen hours a day, and by himself.

He was knocking the crating off a cooking range that had been delivered that afternoon from the Kansas Pacific depot when Luke came around. It was after eleven, going on midnight, when the rattle came at the door. Arn looked up; there was one small window in the front of the store, but Railhead had no street lamps, and the outside world was a bottle of ink.

The old Springfield, loaded, was propped in a corner. Arn took a step toward it and then, with a self-conscious grin, went to the door empty-handed.

"Looks like cotton-picking time in Dixie, Massa," Luke said as he came in. "You really got up a sweat."

The night was close; there was heat lightning on the horizon.

"There's a bathtub at the Cattleman's Rest," Luke said, with a delicate gesture of the thumb and forefinger toward his nose.

"At two dollars a night," Arn grunted.

"That's for those wild-eyed cow nurses from Texas," Luke said. "For friends, seventy-five cents."

Arn pointed to the blanket roll on top of one of the counters.

"That comes with the place. And a hard bed is good for the back." He touched himself and grinned wryly. "My poor old back."

Hands in his pockets, Luke wandered around the room. His Wellington boots clicked against the rough plank floor, and Arn noticed for the first time a new touch. The carved handle of a long-bladed knife was visible above the top of the right boot. Luke's coat was maroon and his pants were the color of heavy cream.

"You're just about the purtiest thing that ever walked around a hardware store, you know it?"

"I *am* the purtiest," Luke said grinning. He stopped in front of the half-uncrated cookstove, opened the lid, looked in the oven, and then swung the door shut again. "Funny hardware store."

"How?"

"Look at what you got. Stoves, both for heating and cooking. What's this, harness? And singletrees and doubletrees—where are all the work horses coming from? Lanterns, Tinware." He stopped in front of two heavy crates. "This is more like it. What are you carrying?"

"Shotguns, mostly. A few Winchesters and Remingtons—game rifles."

"No side arms?"

"There are a few .38's there. But I figure the future of this business isn't in the revolver market."

"What makes you think so? Arn, you know that the first thing these cow waddies do when they hit town is start spending money, and one of the first things they'll spend it on is a fancy gun." He propped his foot against a case and patted the top of his boot. "And lay in some stickers; Indians will give their soul for a good knife. Some dressed-up saddles might be a good idea, too."

"Maybe you should be in the hardware business."

"Maybe I should." His dark eyes flashed across the shelves again. He chuckled. "Pots and pans and doubletrees."

"Luke, around Hays City they got these Russian immigrants with a new kind of winter wheat. They call it Red Turkey. You plant it in the fall, and you can graze it in the spring for a while. It takes the drought a lot better and it mills out good. And it grows like buffalo grass."

"What about the cattle trade?"

"The cattle trade will move on anyhow. It moved out of Abilene and Ellsworth, didn't it? And they're better off because it did."

"I doubt it," Luke said. "The day that this place is full of grangers and oxen is a day I don't want to see."

Arn laughed.

"Luke, what do you think you were but a granger—two short weeks ago?"

Luke was moving again, wandering toward the rear of the store with his hands in the pockets of the cream-colored pants.

"Are you still sweet on Mattie?"

The question was quiet but quick, and it caught Arn like a whip across his shoulders. He made no attempt to answer for a long moment and Luke stood without turning, looking toward the rear of the store.

"I guess any man with salt in his blood who knows Mattie is sweet on her, at least some."

Luke came around.

"You been talking to her? About me?"

"No. I've only seen her a couple of times. You know how things have been with me and the hardware business."

"Somebody," Luke said softly, "has been poisoning the well. She's gone and got herself a job with Doc Chubb, and all of a sudden things look different. I didn't pay much mind when she got all fussy and womanlike when she got here. This looks like—like a permanent change of plans."

He took three steps, and they brought him so close to Arn that their faces were less than a foot apart.

"I don't like it," Luke said.

"I can't blame you. But get it straight; I had nothing to do with it. Mattie's got a mind of her own. I doubt if anybody makes it up for her."

"They'd better not try."

They stood uncertainly, facing each other, for a moment. Then some of the stiffness seemed to slide out of Luke; he dropped his hand on Arn's elbow as he went to the door.

"Look," Arn said, "she came out here to marry you. You're the kind of man you wanted to be for her. What are you waiting for?"

"The purtiest man in Railhead," Luke said. "That's what we decided, wasn't it? See you later, chappie."

They were waiting for him, and jumped him the instant he stepped outside; the grunt, the half-smothered shout came as soon as the door closed. Arn, who had started for the back of the store, whirled to the window. But he was in the light, the rest of the world in blackness; all he could see was his own reflection in the glass. He grabbed up the Springfield and, swinging it by the barrel, crashed out the hanging lamp. Then he pulled open the door.

There had been no gunfire. The blackness was a tangle of squirming shapes, with the dust rising, and besides the grunts and curses, somebody was laughing. There were fist-noises: the soft, cruel thud of knuckles against flesh and bone.

"All the way, boys," drawled a voice. "Clear down to the nub."

At these quarters, with this kind of light, it was impossible to use the Springfield as a gun. Arn caught a glimpse of a hat that was neither white nor flat-topped and, still holding the rifle by the barrel, swung it overhead and down. The hat and the man under it melted.

Then somebody drove a shoulder into his gut with paralyzing force and Arn pitched forward, swinging wildly as he fell. Knuckles caught him across the mouth, an elbow banged his ribs. It was like falling into a barrel of wildcats. He jabbed with knees and flailed with his arms; he did a good deal of damage until a boot caught him underneath the chin. After that, he lost interest for a while. He felt nothing and heard things but distantly. Somebody was laughing.

When he was finally able to sit up and see a little, they had gone. He slid backward and his shoulders stopped against a wall. The street was to his right. Somebody had pulled him around to the west side of the store.

But he was not alone. Suddenly he was aware of heavy breathing close to his ear, breathing with a painful grunt in it, almost like a snore.

"Luke?"

The reply was a mumble. Painfully, Arn got to his feet; his eyes were working now. Luke was sprawled at his feet, face down. Arn got his hands under his armpits and hauled him upright. Luke was naked as a jay bird.

For a few steps Arn almost dragged him, but he was able to stand alone by the time they fumbled their way into the dark store.

"There's a lantern around here somewhere—"

"Never mind," Luke said fiercely. "I don't want any light."

"We better have a look at you; you might be hurt."

"I'm not hurt!" The voice was almost savage, and Luke's fingers dug into his shoulders. "You keep shut about this. Nobody makes a fool of me. This never happened, do you hear me? Keep shut!"

"All right, but it won't do any good," Arn said. "You think the waddies who did it are going to keep shut? This'll be all over town."

"Shut up!"

Luke was too weak to throw much of a punch, but it still was hard enough, coming out of the darkness, to rock Arn backward. A flare of anger went through him; he cocked his own fist, then let it drop.

"All right, Luke," he said quietly. "You want some clothes?"

No more talk passed between them. Luke got into the clothes in a hurry. Arn saw the door come open and the slender figure, a shadow against the lighter shadows, limp painfully away on bare feet.

34

THE KANSAS PACIFIC RAILROAD LAID RAILHEAD OPEN LIKE A knife, and on one side was the bank and the Methodist Church and the other enterprises that went with these symbols of the steadfast, the honorable, the washed and combed. On the other side of the tracks was Joyville. If the bank and the depot and the stock pens were the beating heart of Railhead, Joyville was where the blood came most furiously to the surface; Joyville was where the pulse was fastest, and where the flush showed.

There was not a single stone building, from the ground to the roof, in the entire section. It had grown too fast. Joyville had popped out of the prairie like a slightly rancid mushroom when the first trail herd arrived. Its population was made up of what Railhead's weekly newspaper liked to call the *demimonde*. And it was dedicated to *le sport*.

It had fights: badger fights, cock fights, dog fights, exhibitions of the manly art of self-defense. These were above and beyond the unscheduled fights which eddied through its streets every summer night. It had games, for the boys who liked to play games: chuck-a-luck and faro and keno and sledge, and always poker and dice, poker and dice. It had refreshments, an astonishing variety of them: whiskey from Missouri and Kentucky and Pennsylvania, rum from Jamaica, honest Madeira from an island in the ocean, cognac from France—and virtuoso bartenders who knew how to make the most of these ingredients. It had Professor Davis, who did legerdemain, pulled teeth, and read the bumps on people's heads; and the Armless Wonder, a gentleman who could write documents with his educated toes. It had Soiled Doves for dove-fanciers (they were always listed that way on the police blotter when, once a month, they were herded into court and fined ten dollars apiece). Joyville had everything.

One of its better establishments was the Paris Girl Saloon. The Paris female existed only on the establishment's sign, but there she was pretty spectacular. The sign had been cut to shape; it was almost life-size, and the lady was suspended from the ridgepole, overhanging the street, by a hook set in the top of her red enameled head. To strangers who saw the silhouette after dark, swinging slightly in a prairie breeze, the effect was startling—something as if an underdressed young woman had hanged herself and had been frozen in mid-kick by the rope.

Major Elihu Watson, of course, was not startled at all when he woke up at seven o'clock in the morning and saw the Paris Girl. He had seen her many times before from approximately this same position. The Major had slept on the sidewalk. Not in the gutter; on the plank walk which was some six inches above the level of the street. He had no recollection of going to sleep, but he had apparently made preparations; his coat and vest were folded under his head, and his boots stood beside him. Nobody had disturbed them. The Major was well-known in Joyville.

His head was fuzzy and his stomach moved uncomfortably in the cold hollow above his belt, but the Major had learned to live with these inevitable consequences.

"Good morning, girl from Paris," he yawned. He struggled to a sitting position. "Good morning, lovely messenger from the land beyond—"

Then, for the first time, his eyes began to function properly. They became very wide.

"Haw!"

The great whoop of laughter from the Major's throat echoed and rattled along Joyville's street, deserted and dead at this time of morning. The Major scrambled to his feet, the laughter rolling out of him like water out of a jug.

"Hey!" he yelled. "Come and see! Come one, come all!"

His laughter rose; he flailed his arms helplessly against his sides, like a rooster on a fence. Down the street a window in the Rose Garden came up; a head came out. Other windows opened, then doors.

The Major sat down again, right in the middle of the boardwalk.

"Look at it!" he gasped to the world. "Look at it! *Haw!*"

LUKE RATTLED THE DOOR OF THE HARDWARE STORE ABOUT nine o'clock. Arn was in the middle of excelsior and cardboard again, and it took him awhile to untangle himself. There was no glass in the door, and so he had no idea of the identity of his visitor until he unlatched. Then, unconsciously, he took a fast step backward.

"Brought back your stuff," Luke muttered, and thrust a rolled bundle toward him. "Don't worry; I'm not looking for a fight."

He was in his own clothes again, but the effect was not quite as natty as usual. He wore moccasins, not high boots, and the black broadcloth trailed off to an embarrassed end at his ankles. The cuffs of his white shirt hung open, without links.

"I've got some coffee," Arn said. "Left over; it can be reheated."

"I can use it."

There was a purple welt along one side of Luke's face and a molehill growing on his left eye. His walk was painfully cautious.

36

For a moment they looked at each other without speaking; an invisible line stretched between them. Then Luke broke it.

"Wanted to say I'm sorry," he said. "Guess I hit you last night, didn't I? You'd think by that time we'd both had a bellyful of hitting."

"I guess we better not talk about it."

"Why not?"

"Because when I get to talking about last night, and to thinking about it," Arn said, "I'm liable to laugh." He ran his eye up and down his visitor again. "Just looking at you now, I'm liable to laugh."

After a moment one side of Luke's mouth lifted and the grin flashed through his puffy lips.

"By Judas," he said, "I guess it is funny, in a way."

The buggy that moved across the window had yellow spokes and red hubs, and Mr. Columbine was banging the door almost before they stopped turning. Arn let him in, but he went past Arn as if a wind had blown the door open.

"I've been all over town," he said. "What the devil happened to your clothes?"

"A bunch jumped me in the dark and took 'em," Luke muttered.

"Well, they've been found." Arn had never seen the lawyer angry before; the lines around his mouth, soft and almost laughing when Mr. Columbine was looking casual, or shrewd, or pleased, stood out like hard brackets. "Over in Joyville. We're going over there."

"What for?" Luke said, a little bewildered. "They're ruined anyhow; Joyville can have them."

"We're going to go over and get them back," Columbine said, hammering the words one at a time. "They're strung up on some saloon. Half the town's been over to look already. Laughing their heads off."

He took a couple of steps nearer.

"I said they're laughing, Luke. Cow-prods with hang-overs and grangers with hay in their ears. Dammit, boy, you're the marshal of this town."

"Let them laugh; we been laughing ourselves," Arn said. "Could I interest you in some coffee, lawyer?"

"I've changed my mind," Luke said stiffly. "I don't think it's funny any more."

"We can go in the buggy," Columbine said. "You got to realize I'm more or less involved in this, too. I set you up in this town."

He started toward the door.

"Wait a minute."

Luke pushed his coat back, showing the empty spot where the gun ordinarily rode.

37

"You're just going after a suit of clothes," Arn said sharply. "It won't get that serious."

"Not at all," the lawyer said. He had relaxed; the lines around his mouth were almost laughing again, and he reached up and pawed the clump of grey hair out of his eyes. "Anyhow, there's a carbine in the buggy."

THE CREAM-COLORED PANTS HAD BEEN FITTED ON THE wooden Parisienne's legs, and the coat slid onto her inviting arms. There was no sign of the fine black boots or the gun, but the white hat was hooked on a toe. The breeze swung her gently back and forth, and she smiled an enameled smile at the citizens.

There were at least twenty of them smiling back at her when the buggy pulled up—Soiled Doves and section hands off the KP and Texas cowhands whose eyes were still sticky with sleep. When the buggy stopped, the chatter died. There was a moment of complete silence, broken only by the faint sounds of feet getting set to run. The good burghers of Joyville were experts at the fast breakaway when trouble started.

"Lawyer," said a voice, almost from beneath the wheels of the buggy, "you're going to have to buy your rooster some new feathers."

Major Elihu Watson was sitting at the edge of the walk, his heels pulled under him and his greasy black hat stuck on the back of his head. Without looking twice, Arn, who had also come in the buggy, knew that the Major was fermented all the way this time.

"Hello, Elihu," Columbine said. "You would be right in the middle of this, wouldn't you?"

"As a spectator only. Marshal, you look as if somebody had just shook you out of a sack."

He threw back his head and howled. The chorus picked it up, but it died again as Luke stepped down from the buggy.

"You think it's funny?"

"Hilarious," the Major said. He scuffled to his feet and, weaving a little, faced Luke.

Arn moved quickly around the end of the buggy, sliding in between the two men.

"Major, you look kind of tired to me. Let's see if we can't find you a bed somewhere."

"I'm as alert as a bull in flytime," the Major said.

"Come on." Arn tugged at the arm.

"Wait a minute." Luke's left hand dropped back to the floor of the buggy. "You just stand aside, chappie. I came here to get my clothes. The Major's going to crawl up and get them for me."

38

"Luke, he's wall-eyed. Don't pick on him."

"You let me do it my way," Luke said, speaking to Arn alone. His voice was almost a whisper. "I won't hurt him. But this thing's got to be faced out." His voice lifted. "Come on, you old billy goat. Climb."

"We'll make a deal," Watson said. "I'll get a ladder, and you do the climbing."

"It won't take a ladder." Luke indicated the posts supporting the porch roof. "You even got your boots off; you're all set."

The Major opened his mouth to speak again, but the words didn't come out. The Major fell apart. The defiance went out of his eyes; they opened wide, like a frightened kid's. Suddenly, as if he'd abruptly gone sober, the Major was scared and all the man drained out of him. Arn looked the other way. His stomach was a cold lump.

There was no laughter in the crowd now, no noise at all. There was a kind of sullen pity on their faces, and some of the eyes that turned toward Luke were hot with anger. Luke leaned back against the buggy, his left hand still behind him on the floor.

A couple of them gave Watson a boost. He was hurrying now, clawing at the smooth wood of the post with both hands, like a frightened cat on a slippery tree. An indistinguishable mumble of words came from his lips.

It's gone all wrong, Arn thought. *This isn't helping anything; they aren't laughing now, but it was better when they were, a lot better.*

The Major had his hands on the eaves, and, with a final boost, rolled onto the roof. He stood up, but the sight of the ground was apparently too much for him. He went back to his hands and knees and crawled over to the sign. He removed the hat from the lady's toe and went to work on the trousers. They stuck; he pulled desperately, and there was a sound of ripping cloth. He rocked back on his heels and dropped his face to his hands. When he looked up again, he seemed a man who had awakened in a strange room.

"What the hell am I doing?" he said. The words were clear and sharp.

Arn had never seen the Major stand as straight as he did now. His shoulders were back and his heels were together.

"Malette!" he shouted down at Luke. "Malette, I don't crawl for anybody!"

He brushed his coattail back and reached for the old Army revolver. It seemed to bounce from the holster into his palm, and the muzzle was just bearing down when the carbine cracked. Luke had fired from the hip. He still stood with his back to the buggy.

39

The Major jarred backward a step and then caught himself. The gun hand dropped to his side, but he got it up again.

"Bang," he said hoarsely. "Bang, bang."

The gun dropped and then he followed it, pitching headfirst over the eaves into the dust of the street.

"THE SHOT," DOCTOR HOMER CHUBB SAID, WHILE HE WASHED his hands, "was not fatal. Just an ordinary wound. Dozens of men hurt worse are walking the streets of this town today."

"This one," Columbine said, indicating the table, "seems to be moderately dead."

Columbine sat in Doc's big chair, one leg hung loosely over the arm, one hand busy with a cheroot, the other waving while he talked. Arn sat on the bench against the wall with Mattie beside him. Luke did not sit at all; mostly he moved, back and forth along the length of the room. He had not spoken a word since they brought the Major in.

"The slug cracked the thigh bone and slid off, up into the meaty part of the hip," Doc said. "Nothing deadly about it. But the rascal had been pickled in whiskey for years, he didn't know what solid food tasted like. His heart was low and his liver probably gone. Shock killed him." Doc rolled down his cuffs and put the links through. "A nice hard punch to the jaw might have done the same thing."

"Sure," Columbine said. "The Major had run out the string, anyhow."

"There's nothing to feel bad about," Doc said, looking at Luke. "Absolutely nothing."

Arn wasn't sure that Luke needed consolation. The blank quiet of his face might have meant anything, but as he watched him pace, Arn remembered something somebody had said:

The fire in his eyes, afterward. As if he'd had a couple of drinks.

"Guess we might as well call this the inquest, while we're at it," Doc said, scratching among the papers on his desk for a pen. "Sound legal, lawyer?"

"Legal enough," Columbine said around the cheroot.

"Then there's something else that maybe ought to be said," Arn said. "It's not important, but I guess it belongs in the evidence." He picked up the Army revolver from the bench beside him. "This gun won't fire. The action's rusted out."

Luke's head snapped up.

"What do you mean it won't fire?"

"Try it." Arn pitched it across to him. "That trigger's as solid as if it had been carved there. It's not loaded, either."

40

Luke turned the gun in his hands. From the tail of his eye Arn saw the girl leaning forward, her hands clenching the edge of the bench.

"What difference does it make?" Luke said. His hands shook, and the words were loud. "He pulled, didn't he?"

"Absolutely," Columbine said.

The marshal moved a couple of steps toward Arn.

"If a man pulls a gun," he said, "am I supposed to go up and make sure it's loaded and that the trigger pulls right before I pull mine?"

Mattie was on her feet; she reached up and took her bonnet from the peg on the wall. There was a wordless exchange between herself and the doctor, and then the door closed behind her. The sound brought Luke around.

"It doesn't make any difference at all about the gun," Arn said patiently. "Only they're putting it down for the record, and I thought maybe it belonged. Am I right?"

Columbine shrugged, and the Doc scratched his pen over the paper again.

"Anybody else got accusations to make?" Luke said.

Arn felt the temper rising in him.

"I'm not accusing you of anything," he said sharply.

"You've got a name for me," Luke said through clenched teeth. "You won't say it, but you're putting down names for me in your head. You didn't like what happened this morning, did you? You look sick at your stomach."

"I am. But it wasn't just the shooting. After it had gone as far as it did, I suppose there was nothing for you to do but shoot. Like you said—he pulled, didn't he?"

Luke didn't hear the last of it. He was gone, and the door closed behind him. In the long interval of silence that followed, Mr. Columbine blew three puffs of smoke, like Indian blanket sign, toward the ceiling. Doc Chubb scratched some more with his pen and then shoved the paper aside.

"I've had a thought, Edward," he said. "We've got a vacancy on the Council now. And we got a brand-new businessman in town. Plans to be permanent. Got sense and a level head."

Columbine's leg slid off the arm of the chair and the last mouthful of smoke trickled through his teeth. He gave Chubb a long, sharp look and then turned toward Arn.

"Well, sure," he said finally. The chuckle that came out seemed a little dry. "How do you feel about civic responsibility, Hendricks?"

"That's election business, isn't it?"

"Mayor appoints until the vacancy can be filled," Doc said. "Heavens knows when we'll get around to that. You know, Edward, this is quite a pair of young men. We already got one of them working for the town. Might as well get the whole team."

"Didn't look like much of a team when Luke walked out," Columbine said.

"He's got the shakes; it'll wear off." A thoughtful shadow passed across Doc's face. "Although that boy—" He shrugged and the smile came back. "Right now, I'm appointing. How about it?"

Arn's impulse was to refuse. The business wasn't altogether set up yet; there was a mountain of work ahead. And Watson had joked about how useless the Council was. The way this town was run—if you could consider it run at all—had little to do with councilmen or even His Honor, Doc Chubb. So far as city government went, Railhead was in a poor way.

Maybe that was why Arn Hendricks nodded his head and grinned back at Doc Chubb and then put out his hand for the ceremonial shaking.

THE HEAT THAT COMES IN A DRY KANSAS SUMMER HAS MUCH in common with the desert. Generally it is clear and light; it does not lie clammily in the secret places of the body, draining out strength and nibbling at the temper and the mind. In Kansas, a man can work in the fields with the temperature well over a hundred and—providing he has sufficient water—work efficiently and almost comfortably.

Nevertheless this heat kills, as effectively as the heat of a flame. The ground takes it up the same way it takes water, and roots of plants cook and shrivel away. No coolness comes with night. The heat accumulates, and if there is no rain, the prairie turns to ash.

By the first of July it was apparent that the emergency corn crop planted on the claim wasn't going to make it, even if it was in bottom ground. Some of it had barely broken through; the best was not six inches. Nevertheless Arn worked at it. For the exercise, maybe, for the sake of the work itself. There was something he liked about the sun beating into him and the sweat streaming down his arms. He came out every Sunday.

They had not given up the claim, although both their interests were now in Railhead. Columbine had made them a nominal offer, on a casual take-it-or-leave-it basis. Luke, completely unconcerned, had left the decision in Hendricks' hands, and it didn't take much deciding. The hardware business was like any other business, unpredictable, but the land was always there.

So on a Sunday afternoon, two days before the Fourth,

Arn hacked away at the rock-hard earth around the pathetic shoots of late corn. The world was deserted, the air completely clear. He saw the puff of dust a long way down the road when he stopped to lift the stone jug of water to his mouth.

It was a buggy, and, pleasantly conscious of the privilege of wasting time if he wanted to, Arn suspended work to watch it come. It left the road at the turn and headed across the sunburnt grass toward the soddie. A woman was doing the driving, but he didn't recognize Mattie until she was almost in the lot.

"Where'd you get the rig?"

"It's the Reverend's," she answered as he handed her down. "He doesn't like to drive on Sunday; I think maybe he feels it's the devil's work."

"Then how come he lets you drive it?"

"I think he's figuring on saving me one of these days, and maybe he wants to lift a real burden while he's at it." She giggled; not foolishly, but still it was a giggle. It struck Arn that it was the first time he'd heard that sound since she arrived in Railhead. "Good heavens, the dust! I suppose the next question is why I drove all the way out here in the first place?"

"I suppose."

She moved slowly toward the soddie.

"I just wanted to see it. I never have, you know. The place I thought I was coming to when I left for Kansas. May I go in?"

Arn went ahead and unfastened the bolt which he had recently rigged on the door. Inside the room was cool and shadowy.

"One thing about a sod roof," Arn said. "It keeps the heat out."

She looked at the tin-and-limestone stove, at the bureau; she sat solemnly in each of the two crude chairs and looked down the chimney of the coal-oil lamp brought all the way from Ohio. Then she slid back the curtains and looked in the alcove. She stood there for maybe a full minute, looking and saying nothing.

"I'm afraid it's not much," Arn said apologetically.

"It's wonderful," she said. "I—I could have been very happy here."

She turned her back on it and moved away. She wore no bonnet today—that must have given the Reverend a bit of a blow, Arn thought—and the yellow elegance of her hair was in one twisted knot, low on her neck.

"I guess I did a pretty awful thing, Arn," she said, and smiled wryly. "I wanted to tell you about it before Luke did.

43

Anyway you hear it, though, it turns out that I'm a bull-headed woman."

Deep in his bones Arn Hendricks knew what she was going to say, but he didn't know whether the news pleased him or made him angry. In a way, maybe it even frightened him.

"Luke's been—well, a lot more attentive lately. But not in the way a woman wants. He's been after me to set a date; he's impatient, as if I was unfinished business. As if he had other things to do, and other things to think about. So I set a date."

"You—what?"

It wasn't what he expected, after all.

"I told him that the day he put his guns away and stopped marshaling, I'd marry him." Her eyes fell, searching her hands; she shook her head. "Maybe that wasn't honest; maybe I wouldn't have gone through with it, even then. But it's what I told him."

"What did he say?"

"The cat took his tongue and he stared at me just—just as if he hadn't heard me at all. We were standing on the porch at the Reverend's and I stood there, hollow and cold inside, and waited for him to say something, do something. Then I started feeling foolish and maybe even a little mad."

"Sure," Arn said thickly. "You would have felt a lot better if he'd gone to pieces, wouldn't you?"

"No!" she gasped. "I didn't want to hurt him. No, Arn!"

"Whether you wanted to or not, it must have hurt like hell."

The sudden brightness in her eyes was overflowing in streaks down her cheeks, but she did not lower her head.

"Arn," she said, "I'm hurt as much as anybody in this."

"You came out here for a wedding. Did you plan to marry a man, or the job he held?"

Arn did not know where his words came from now. Not from his feelings; from somewhere else, from some odd corner of his mind that stood apart and spoke for itself.

"The man I came to marry isn't here any more!" she burst out. "Arn, I've never been so lonely in my life."

He took two steps and his arms were around her. She went limp against his body, her forehead in the angle of his neck and shoulder. His hands moved against her ribs and over her back in clumsy, comforting motions. And then she was no longer limp. Her fingers dug into the muscles of his arm.

He pushed her head back and brought his mouth down hard on her half-open lips, and the odd corner of his mind that spoke for Luke was blotted out altogether.

When he let her go, he looked around at the familiar room

44

as if he'd never seen it before. Mattie stood a step away, her back to him, her shoulders moving with heavy breath. She might have been crying. He reached out a hand and gently turned her around.

"It never happened, if that's the way you want it," he said. "It never happened at all."

"But it did," she said.

She wasn't crying.

She left immediately, and there was no more talk between them. Except for the last moment, when he handed her into the buggy. As she unfastened the lines looped around the dashboard, he said, "What if I fell in love with you?"

Her hands tightened on the leather until her knuckles showed white; she refused to look at him.

"Don't," she said. "Please don't."

She smacked the lines across the rump of the Reverend's big horse, and the buggy jerked away. Arn stood where he was, not moving. He stood there until she was gone, and the fine trace of dust puffed by the wheels was the only sign that she had been there at all.

THERE WAS NO RAIN ON THE GLORIOUS FOURTH, BUT RAIL-head was nevertheless wet. The proprietor of the Paris Girl Saloon set three barrels on wooden horses on the sidewalk, with a tin cup chained to each and a man with a shotgun standing on either side of the setup. There was a tin box with a slot in front of each barrel. The customer filled his cup and pitched a dime into the box. This arrangement not only kept traffic moving at a better clip but also inclined the celebrant toward violence on the outside rather than amid the fragile furniture in the interior.

There were numerous sporting events. Horse racing went on all day long on the improvised oval behind Joyville. A boxing match, involving a gentleman purported to be the champion of Kansas City, Missouri, was held at high noon. A four-piece band played and City Attorney Edward Colum-bine spoke upon the subject of Liberty for one hour and forty-five minutes. Two Lone Star lads were inspired to demonstrate. in a friendly spirit of international good will, the favorite sport of their Mexican neighbors with a longhorn steer borrowed from the shipping pens, and one of them was gored through the thigh.

And the Methodist church had a box supper.

This event began at five o'clock in the afternoon, in the street immediately in front of the church and adjoining the parsonage. An auction platform was set up; the rough benches which served as pews in the church and some trellis tables

45

were available for seating. Most of the customers, however, were expected to sit upon the lawn, and the buffalo grass had been carefully scythed.

The auctioneer did his calling against a background of racket from Joyville, where the spirit of liberty was still going strong. The Reverend Minner stood beside him on the platform, and held the boxes up one at a time, looking owl-eyed and uncomfortable. The Reverend's chief job was the stimulation of business by giving cues; when a young lady's offering came under the hammer, he'd give an ecclesiastical wink to the appropriate young man.

Item number eleven was a rectangular box done up in white paper with a light-green ribbon around it and three black-eyed Susans on top. Arn had seen that ribbon many times before around a coil of corn-colored hair. The Reverend Minner stood on tiptoe and, with an encouraging smile, threw a wink toward the back of the crowd. Luke stood by himself, his coat open, the private one-sided smile on his lean face.

"Two dollars," Luke said.

Arn cleared his throat and took a deep breath.

"Three," he said, somewhat more loudly than necessary.

"I got three," the auctioneer said.

"Three-fifty," Luke said.

"Four."

The crowd liked it. They buzz-buzzed and stretched their necks and tittered. The grin on Luke's face looked as if it were pasted on.

"Seven-fifty," he said.

Arn saw Mattie, in the front row, turn around. She threw him a look of sudden concern, her grey eyes troubled. Arn looked past her, right at the auctioneer.

"Ten dollars," he shouted.

The crowd went *whoooooooo!*

"I've got ten! Ten, ten, ten." The auctioneer waved his gavel. "I'm liable to take ten, unless the long arm of the law interferes. Marshal?"

They were all looking at Luke now. After a moment he lifted his hat and swung it across his body in a bow. The ladies fluttered.

Arn gave the Reverend the greenbacks, got his reward, and then came to claim his lady. He led her into a pool of shade cast by the cottonwoods in front of the parsonage. The full skirt of the light-green dress made a circle when she sat.

"Cherry pie?" he said.

"Green apple," she said absently. "Arn—I wish you hadn't."

46

"Well, maybe I shouldn't have. Ten dollars is a lot of money, but I figure you're only young once."

"I didn't mean that. Luke didn't like it. They were laughing at him. It's not good to make a fool out of Luke."

Arn gave her a long look.

"Maybe I was making a fool of myself," he said.

The grey eyes came very close.

"I don't want you to have trouble with Luke, not bad trouble."

Arn pulled one of the black-eyed Susans from the cluster and threaded it through the buttonhole of his lapel.

"Listen to me, Mattie. I figure he'll find out, and he might as well start today—"

The high black boots were moving over the grass toward them, and they eased away from each other in self-conscious silence.

"No fair," Luke said. "You must have heard about that chuck-a-luck game I was in last night, chappie, and my weakened financial condition."

"Nope," Arn said. "I just happen to like pie—and a pretty woman."

"The lawn is full of women with pies."

Arn came slowly to his feet.

"I happen to like this woman better than any of the others," he said quietly. "Like to sit down and join us, Luke?"

There was not a flicker of movement anywhere on Luke's face, and he did not speak, but the silence that grew between them was loud enough to drown out any words.

"There's a whole pie," Mattie said finally. "Sandwiches, and enough deviled eggs for a crew of threshers—"

"It would make me look pretty silly in this town if somebody took my girl away from me," Luke said. "Especially a man like you, chappie."

"What kind of man am I?" Arn said.

"The kind with sleeve protectors and a pen behind his ear. A man who chases nickels. A man with soft hands who doesn't know the butt of a gun from the muzzle. Competition would look bad for me. I'm afraid we can't have it."

"I expect she'll do the deciding."

"I wouldn't trust any woman to do that," Luke said. "You're going to decide it, and I've just made up your mind for you."

"I make up my own mind. Get it straight, Luke."

The grin suddenly split Luke's face wide open, and the fine teeth flashed like a blade in the sunlight.

"Then make it up to one more thing. You're going to have to start dressing right."

"What does that mean?"

"The man who goes around this town without iron on his hip," Luke said, "is half-naked."

Then easing down until he sat on his heels, he lifted one corner of the box lid and peeked inside.

"Deviled eggs I can't stand," he said. "But I could use some of that pie."

LUKE DID MOST OF THE EATING AND ALL OF THE TALKING; HE was as casual, as relaxed, as if they had talked of nothing but the weather. Arn had seen this in him many times—watched the tension build until Luke was like a spring wound too tight and then, with a single word or smile or gesture, uncoil and become loose and easy. There was something oddly frightening about it.

They were almost finished when McCloy came up. Two fiddlers and a guitar player were on the platform now, and some of the crowd had gathered around. It was going dark.

"Company," Arn said softly. "I didn't know he was around here any more."

McCloy looked as if he'd been dressed to the hilt when he started, but the festivities of the day had been a little too much for him. His claw-hammer coat was caked with dust, and the embroidered vest hung open. The murderous-looking shotgun with the short barrels was looped over his shoulder; when he walked, his arm rode against it, to keep it from bouncing against his body.

Luke came to his feet like a cat.

"I bring," said McCloy, "the greetings of the season." He removed his hat. "Happy Independence Day. Today I like everybody. I even like the state of Kansas."

He wasn't looking for a fight, Arn decided, and from the tail of his eye he saw Luke relax a little as he came to the same conclusion.

"I even like grangers," McCloy said, "and I came to say hello. Of course, you grangers aren't exactly grangers any more, are you? These days you wear neckties." He bent toward Mattie. "Ma'am, you can consider yourself lucky to know two young men who started out being nothing and in such a short time got to be something. If being town men is something. Godamighty, you're a pretty woman. My name's McCloy, and I don't believe I've had the pleasure."

"You haven't and you won't," Luke said. McCloy grinned at him amiably.

"You're looking kind of elegant yourself," Arn said. "How come you're still in this country? Aren't they running long-horns out of the Panhandle any more?"

"I'm doing fine up here. I guess I'll stay a while. I move around; Abeline, Ellsworth—although they're pretty dead now—Salina, Dodge. Dodge City looks like it might turn into quite a town."

"You move around," Luke repeated sardonically. "I can imagine. They tell me the horse market is pretty good now, and that cavalry outfit at Fort Miller is practically afoot after some smart fellas hit them last week. And there's always beef. Trail boys coming in here tell me they lose a lot to rustlers."

"Conditions in Kansas," McCloy said, "are very unsettled. Ma'am, I hope you weren't planning to throw the rest of that pie away?"

"Don't give him anything, Mattie," Luke said. "He's just leaving."

"There's a lot of it left. Mr. McCloy might as well have some, in the spirit of the occasion."

The Texan grinned triumphantly at Malette and reached for the plate which she handed up. His arm was out full length as he did so, and his sleeve pulled back. The cuff was soiled and sweaty, but the thing that caught the eye was the cuff link—a small but perfect opal, set in gold.

Luke's sharp intake of breath and the smack of his palm against the gun butt came at the same time. An instant later the muzzle cleared leather.

"McCloy," he said, "I want my cuff links."

For an instant all of them froze, like children in a parlor game. The shotgun was around the curve of McCloy's hip, and he was smart enough to know that he would never finish a movement toward it. Besides, the pie was in his outstretched right hand.

So he threw the pie.

The range was point-blank, not more than two feet; he pitched it underhand. Dough and liquid and slippery apples smacked into Luke's face, and then McCloy threw himself backward, going for the shotgun.

Arn threw himself blindly, head down, throwing his left arm out to catch the gun hand. He caught McCloy's wrist and knocked it upward. The hammer action on the twelve-gauge had been filed fine, and the impact jarred both barrels off at the same time. The blast that splintered into the branches of the cottonwood tree sounded like a cannon.

McCloy stumbled backward for a couple of steps and fell, but he was up again like a rubber ball—up and running. He was a swerving shape among the crowd in an instant; they scattered frantically, the women screaming with terror. Arn caught a glimpse of McCloy breaking into the open.

Luke fired twice, and both shots kicked dust beneath McCloy's feet.

"Luke!" Mattie shouted.

In the frightened attempt to take cover, each member of the crowd took his own direction. People charged into each other, ran each other down; the wiser ones dived for the sod and flattened themselves, but the panic was too strong in most of them. Arn caught a glimpse of the Reverend Mr. Minner on the dead run for the church, a screaming child under each arm.

When he saw McCloy again, the cowman had filled his hand from a shoulder holster inside his coat, and an instant later a slug smacked into the cottonwood not a foot from Arn's head. Another one followed it.

"Stop it, stop it, stop it!"

The voice was Mattie's. Luke stood with his feet apart, like a man on the deck of a rolling ship, the six gun at eye level, firing when he caught a glimpse of the claw-hammer coat. McCloy answered twice more; the slugs were wild. There was a good deal of screaming in the crowd, but one thin shriek hung for an instant above the rest.

And then, suddenly, there was quiet. From the street was the sound of hooves in a hurry. The Reverend Mr. Minner came lurching across the lawn toward the cottonwood, his glasses gone, his face an open-mouthed mask of shock.

"Marshal," he said, "what—what—"

The thin shriek rang out again and hung over the sudden quiet of Railhead, and then again and again.

THE BOY WHO WAS KILLED WAS AN ELEVEN-YEAR-OLD, JUAN Gonzales, the son of a Mexican teamster who worked with the track gangs of the Kansas Pacific. He was shot through the lungs. Doc Chubb gave him one hard-eyed glance, gave instructions about removal of the body, headed Mattie toward the shrieking mother, and then turned to his other patients. There were a lot of them. The parade through the little office over the bank went on for almost four hours.

Arn helped handle traffic. He held innumerable hands and made soothing noises until they became idiotic noises to his own ears; he lugged ladies with sprained ankles around like sacks of flour; he peered knowingly, without knowing anything at all, at gashes and chipped teeth. When the last of them was gone he fell into one of the stiff-backed chairs in the tiny outer office and stared blankly at the window that opened on nothing.

There is a romantic tradition that beautiful women have about them the most elegant of odors, an aura of lavender or at least of new-mown hay. The odor that followed Mattie through the door as she came out was raw and pungently medical.

"All through?" Arn asked.

"With the live ones," she said. "He's being a coroner now —probing for the bullet. I decided I wasn't up to it."

"The bullet—"

Arn looked at her with an unspoken question large in his eyes.

"It wasn't Luke," she said. "At least, he doesn't think so; from the looks of the wound, it came from a little gun." She made a face, and her next words were completely empty of feeling. "Does it make any difference?"

"It does," Arn said grimly. "Because somebody's going to be brought to the law about this, if I have anything to say about it."

"McCloy?"

"If it wasn't Luke, it was McCloy."

After a moment she laughed, and it was not a pleasant sound.

"The hard light of justice in your eyes. And Luke's afire with justice, too, I'll bet, pounding the prairie out there with those men he deputized. Do you realize that if the boy had taken a step the other direction he probably would have caught it from the other gun? I'm going home."

She moved toward the door, and Arn came to his feet.

"Alone," she said.

She stopped with her hand on the knob and turned back to him. The delicate green dress was crumpled and soiled, and part of the ripped hem dragged the floor.

"Luke's going to kill you someday," she said. "You know that, don't you? Unless you kill him first."

"Mattie, you're too tired to make sense," Arn said sharply. "I'll take you home and you get to bed and forget about things."

"I'll go home alone," she said, and closed the door behind her.

He sat there for a moment and then went inside and joined Chubb. He did not know why; he had nothing to talk about with Doc. But the only place to go was the darkened store with the bedroll in the rear, and this night would have to grow a good deal older before the thought of bed had any attraction for Arn. Every muscle in his body was tight with fatigue, and his mind had a dread of the kind of loneliness that would make it feed upon its own thoughts.

Doc had finished; the sheet was full-length over the table

again (it struck him with ironic force that he had never been in this room when that table was unoccupied) and the round little physician was squinting through a magnifying glass.

"It's a thirty-two, all right," he said. "Pocket gun of some kind. Not that it makes a great deal of difference."

"That's what Mattie said. Just that."

"Did you take her home? That girl needs rest."

"She went alone. I tried to talk to her, but she's upset."

"That's right," Doc said. "She's upset." He dropped heavily into his chair, pulling off his glasses, and rubbed his eyes with a thumb and forefinger. Doc was breathing like a man who's been on the dead run. "We'll fix up a warrant tomorrow. Luke and his citizens won't be in until morning, anyhow."

He swung around in his chair and, after fumbling his way through a couple of matches, finally started the coal-oil stove that held the coffeepot.

"You look a little upset yourself," Arn said.

"Me?" Doc said. "I'm the soul of scientific detachment." He turned his face, strangely naked without the spectacles, toward the white-sheeted table. "It's not just the fact that some kid got in the way of a bullet. If it hadn't been a bullet, he might have been kicked in the head by a mule, or come down with the typhoid. But where it happened. At a church supper." He said the words over again, as if they were in an incomprehensible foreign tongue. "Hendricks, do you realize that we never had a church supper in this town before?"

"From the way this one worked out, it looks as if it'll be a while before there's another."

"You miss my meaning, boy. The church supper is a symptom, the same way you are a symptom. The town is doing what it has to do, or die; it's growing up." Doc shifted his position, but his eyes still looked at the wall. "This is my town, boy; I came here right after the survey crews for the KP. The first patient I ever treated had a Cherokee arrow in his arm. This place was seven tents and two shacks. In 'sixty-nine a shipment of, uh, ladies from San Francisco brought Asiatic cholera with them. I fought it for seven weeks and never slept for longer than three hours at a stretch. When that was over, me and this town had grown together like the fingers on a scalded hand, and the only kind of pay anybody could think of was to make me mayor. Then the longhorns came, and we really blossomed."

He shook his head and pulled his spectacles on again.

"And now we've got church suppers getting mixed into a gun fight. The cattle will go; anybody with sense knows that. So the church suppers are going to win."

"Are you like Luke?" Arn asked quietly. "Are you sorry?"

"I told you this was my town, boy."

Doc heaved himself out of the chair and paddled across the room. Looped around a peg on the clothes tree, as they always were when he worked, were the ivory-handled Peacemakers in the black leather holsters. Doc turned them butt-to-barrel, so they fitted together, and wrapped the belt around them. Then he gently put them in the bottom drawer of the desk, shoved it shut, and turned the lock with a small brass key. He took a long breath and let it out slowly.

"And now I suppose I ought to throw this away," he said reflectively, bouncing the key in his hand. "But—"

He tossed it high, and the key turned end-over-end, winking yellow in the light. Doc caught it and stuffed it into the pocket of his worn waistcoat.

"That coffee's hot by now," he said. "Want a cup?"

"No, thanks," Arn said, rising. "Remember, I've got the Grand Opening tomorrow."

"By George, that's right. I'd completely forgot."

"For a while," Arn said, "I almost forgot, myself."

HE NEVER DID KNOW WHEN LUKE AND HIS IMPROMPTU deputies came in; somebody said around daylight. The chase was unsuccessful, except for the recovery of a saddle horse stolen from the street at the time of the shooting; it had stepped into a chuckhole and had to be shot. Two other men had ridden out of town with McCloy.

At the best, as Arn figured it, Luke had spent a backbreaking night in the saddle and had slept only four or five hours upon his return. He was nevertheless clear-eyed and immaculate when he showed up at the store at eleven in the morning.

By that time A. HENDRICKS, STOVES, H'DW'RE, &C had done $19.45 worth of business and given away eighteen of the needle packets he was giving as souvenirs to the first twenty-five ladies. Some of the females who obtained needles under this arrangement might have had trouble qualifying as ladies, but it was no day for petty distinctions. This was a day only for big things, a day for which he had waited a long, long time.

He was selling a lantern to a granger who wore homespun and had Kentucky in his speech when Luke came through the door. Arn looked up automatically when the bell clanged, and for a moment his eyes met Luke's. The marshal smiled, touched the brim of his hat, and then turned with an air of great interest to a display of shovels. When the homesteader left, Luke held the door for him and touched his hat again.

"You the marshal?" the Kentuckian said, stopping in the doorway.

"At your service."

"I've heard a lot of things about you. They tell me that this is one town that's really got law."

"That's the way we intend to keep it," Luke said. "Good day, sir."

He bowed him out, and the store was empty except for the two of them. The heels of the high-shine boots clicked on the planking of the floor as the marshal came back to where Arn stood at the cash drawer.

"I don't think you've got what I want in stock," he said, "but I figure you could order it. How's business, chappie?"

"If it went on like this all the time," Arn said, "I'd get rich." He inspected him with frank astonishment. "Still the purtiest thing that ever walked into a hardware store. From what I hear about that ride last night, most people would have spent the day in bed."

"It gave me an appetite for breakfast." Luke grinned. "And for Mr. McCloy. I'm real hungry to see Mr. McCloy again. He's still got my cuff links."

"It'd suit me if he rode all the way to Mexico City. If I never see anything like that business last night again, it'll be too soon. What is it you want to order, Luke?"

Luke didn't answer for a moment. The grin melted.

"I didn't shoot the boy," he said. "Remember it."

"What was it you—"

"I wouldn't want you thinking I did. I wouldn't want you thinking I was responsible in any way. I want you to have a great respect for me, Arn," Luke said, very softly, the dark eyes probing his face.

"I'd never underestimate you, if that's what you mean."

"It's not exactly what I mean, but maybe it'll do." Luke slid a silver cigar case from his pocket and extracted a cheroot. "I need a pair of Peacemakers, chappie. Like that brace of Doc Chubb's. Think you can get them?"

"I guess so," Arn said, after a moment. He reached for a piece of paper.

"Forty-fours, silver-mounted. Blank ivory handles. I'll get my carving done around here."

He put a match to the end of the cheroot and pulled cautiously. Smoking was a new habit with Luke.

"Maybe you'll be ordering for yourself at the same time," he said.

Hendricks straightened up, a look of angry bewilderment in his eyes.

"Luke, get it straight. I don't intend to tote a gun."

54

"You're a businessman now; you've got property to protect. Anyhow, the people of this town expect you to walk heeled."

"That depends upon the people you're talking about. I'll protect my property the way I want to. And while we're on the subject, be careful of the way you talk around Mattie. She thought you were threatening me last night."

"She did?" Luke said, his eyebrows going up. "What did you think?"

The bell on the door clanged, and an Indian in a buckskin shirt with a feather stuck through his hat came in. Arn came around the corner of the counter arranging the smile, the professional smile for the potential customer.

"I hate to say this," Luke murmured, very thoughtfully, as if he'd been working out answers in his head, "but I don't think you belong out here at all. I think you better go back to Ohio and chase your nickels, because this is no country for a coward. And, chappie, I think you're a coward."

RAILHEAD'S GOVERNING BODY, THE CITY COUNCIL, MET IN THE empty room on the second floor of I. Levine, Groceries and Notions. Actually, most of the official functions of the city were discharged in this room; during the day it served as police court, since it was adjacent to the small stone building that served as a jail. There was a long pine table with half a dozen chairs around it and, behind this, a smaller table on a square platform. The place was lighted by pulley-rigged lamps, and on one wall was the flag of the Republic, the vivid color subdued by a layer of dust. On the other wall was the Great Seal of the state of Kansas.

This was Arn's first council meeting; he had been sworn in by Doc Chubb at the beginning, while the June bugs that came through the unscreened windows buzzed and banged against the lamps. He sat at the end of the table and—for a while, at least—satisfied himself with listening. Luke was present, although not at the table; he sat in a chair cocked on its back legs against the wall.

It didn't take much of an eye to determine one thing in the first fifteen minutes. Mr. Edward Columbine had the city council in his pocket. There were four other members, including Columbine. One was Mr. Ernest Patterson, owner of the biggest of Railhead's two livery stables. He was a heavily built man with pale-blue eyes that were in constant motion, looking nowhere; he still wore a bandage on his hand from the battle with Hamilton Otter, the half-breed who had tried to fire his establishment. Then there was a Mr. Grossinger, a cattle trader, a man with an outsize stomach and the heavy breathing of the asthmatic. Neither of these gentlemen said very much. When they said anything, it was an echo of Edward Columbine.

The fourth member was the Reverend Mr. Minner. The Reverend still looked dazed from the doings of Independence Day.

The early business was routine; authorization to the city attorney to contract and pay for three sets of handcuffs and a set of shackles; authorization to the same gentleman to contract and pay for foodstuffs for the inmates of the jail for the next quarter; a complaint from a Mrs. Jacobs about loud singing and sounds of revelry throughout the night (the Council tittered wearily over this one, as if it were an old familiar); authorization for the city attorney to engage a deputy for the marshal, Mr. Malette, and pay his first month's salary. Mr. Columbine, Arn observed, handled a lot of the city's money. To all these things the Council grunted "Aye" and Mr. Columbine blew thoughtful puffs of smoke at the ceiling.

"I have a piece of business I want to bring up," Doc said slowly, after the list was finished. "Before that, any of you members have anything?"

"I guess I might as well get my feet wet," Arn said, clearing his throat with self-conscious vigor. "Your Honor, this town needs street lights. A lot of our all-night uproar could be eliminated if the whole town wasn't dark." He carefully looked away from Luke. "I know of a case when a citizen was assaulted under cover of darkness and various, uh, valuable possessions lost. Street lights would dress up the place, too; people going through on the KP could get a look at the town."

"Well, that shows civic pride," Mr. Columbine said. "But it's impractical. For one thing, the cowhands would shoot them out as fast as they went up."

"We pay a police force," Arn pointed out.

Minner cleared his throat.

"I rather think lights might be a good idea," he said. "I—I agree with this gentleman."

"Let me make it clear, Reverend," Columbine said heartily. "I agree, too, in principle. But there are a lot of considerations. The most important being that we couldn't afford it."

"Maybe we can," Arn said, fishing in his pocket. "I took the liberty of doing some digging. The maintenance superintendent of the Kansas Pacific was in town yesterday, and we chewed this thing. They buy lamps like the ones at the depot in quantity. The KP's interested in this town, and he thinks they might supply us—if not at cost, at least with a big markdown. Couldn't promise, of course, but we did some general figuring." He consulted the paper. "Around three hundred dollars, not counting labor. I'd be glad to handle the actual negotiations—"

"Oh?" Mr. Columbine said, with a rising inflection.

"—at no cost to the city."

"Of course. But it's still impractical because the town hasn't got the money."

"If we're going to spend that kind of money," Mr. Grossinger said, "we ought to spend it on something practical."

There was a moment's silence and then Arn, looking past Columbine to Doc Chubb, said, "I don't quite understand why we're so poor. This town has a considerable income just from fines, for instance. Disturbing the peace is fifteen dollars. Public drunkenness, riding a horse or other quadruped animal into public or private buildings, assault and battery—there's a regular parade through this police court." He glanced toward Luke. "Am I right, Marshal?"

"Well," Luke said, his eyes moving to Columbine. "Well—"

"Not to mention the matter—you'll excuse me, Reverend —of the Soiled Doves. I believe the ladies are rounded up once a month and fined ten dollars. Making a rough guess, I'd say that was around five hundred dollars a month right there."

"Mr. Hendricks," Columbine said, with an impatient gesture, "if you want to make a careful study of city finances, I'm sure Mr. Grossinger—he's the city treasurer, appointed by His Honor here—would be glad to tell you all about it."

"Glad to," Mr. Grossinger said, and licked his lips.

"Meanwhile, I'll venture that it's the opinion of this group that we can't afford any investment of the kind you mention. Not now, anyhow."

"That's my opinion," Mr. Patterson said, and Mr. Grossinger nodded. The Reverend Minner opened his mouth as if to say something and then closed it again.

Mr. Columbine swung his chair around and dropped his boot heels to the floor with a bang.

"Well, Homer, do we call it a day?"

"Not yet. I've got something here."

The round little man smoothed the paper in front of him with the palms of his hands and looked at them over the tops of his glasses. His face was grave.

"Don't suppose any of us have forgotten what happened on the Fourth," he said. "I've done a lot of thinking about it, and it seems to me—well, I'll read this."

He nervously smoothed the sheet again and then read it, very slowly, sometimes hesitantly, as if he wondered over the fitness of a word. It was put in Doc's approximation of legal language, but its content was simple and clear. It was

57

a proposal to make it illegal, except for established officers of the law, to carry firearms on the streets of Railhead.

Feathers of smoke drifted from the mouth of Columbine, who was staring at Doc with fixed intensity. Mr. Patterson kept looking all over the room, and Grossinger snorted through his asthma. From the tail of his eye Arn saw Luke easing the legs of his chair down to the floor.

"Abilene and Ellsworth have laws like this," Doc Chubb said.

"But without enforcing them. Not until the cattle trade left," Columbine said sharply. "Gentlemen, as a lawyer, I have a great respect for the dignity of the law. And I don't like to see any of it generally flouted, because that leads to disrespect for the whole body of the law."

"I move the adoption of this ordinance," Doc Chubb said, looking past him.

"You can't move it, Homer," Columbine said amiably. "It's like voting; the mayor can't vote unless there's a tie. And he can't introduce a measure."

"Then will somebody—"

"Mr. Hendricks will move it for you," Luke said. "It would take a burden off his soul if somebody passed a law about it."

The rest of them didn't know what he was talking about, of course—although Columbine was probably making a pretty good guess. There was a glint of amusement in his eyes. Arn felt his color coming up. The word "coward" on Luke's lips before had stung like a slap, but he knew it wasn't true. This was different; regardless of the fact he thought Chubb was right, that he had thought of the same thing a dozen times, he could not say so. If he did, the next time Luke used the name he'd be right.

So Arn set his teeth and looked away from Doc Chubb's hopeful look.

"I'll move it!" said the Reverend Minner. He came up like a jack-in-the-box. "I realize that nobody pays any attention to me in this group, except to be polite and watch their language." His mouth worked nervously. "Ordinarily I make no objection; I know little of things like street lights and feeding people in jail. But this is quite different. I make a motion to—" he pointed to the sheet of paper in front of Chubb, "to that effect."

"We need a second," Doc said.

"Dammit, Homer," Columbine said amiably, "this proposition would be almost impossible to enforce. And—just speaking personally, you understand—I think it's against the whole tradition and spirit of the town. I know this town, gentlemen;

it's in my blood, and I flatter myself that the reverse holds, too."

Another one whose soul is tied to Railhead, Arn thought. *You'd think this town was a pretty woman.*

"I want this thing to come to a vote," Doc Chubb said stubbornly. "I want it on record. And I need a second."

His eyes moved to Arn; intent, demanding. Luke had cocked his chair against the wall again, the one-sided grin splitting his dark face. There was a long silence.

"Hendricks?"

The silence hung.

"Then the motion dies for lack of a second," Doc Chubb said dully. He got up and kicked back his chair. "So far as I'm concerned, meeting's adjourned."

He headed for the door without looking back.

"There's some information I think you should have," said a voice at Arn's shoulder. He found himself in step with the Reverend Minner. "I believe you have some sort of, ah, affiliation with our guest, Miss Larson?"

"We've known each other for a long time, if that makes an affiliation."

"Did you know she's planning to leave? She was packing her belongings when I came to meeting tonight. I suppose that means the morning train."

"No," Arn said, after a moment. "I didn't know that."

"The girl's very unhappy. I'm uncomfortable about her. If she's determined to go, why, that's her own affair. But—" He made a helpless gesture. "I'd prefer for her to leave with a smile. I suppose that sounds like something a minister would say, but perhaps you know what I mean."

"Reverend, could I go along home with you? I'd like to talk to her."

"It might help. You understand, though, that there's a rule about the use of the parlor. Not after nine thirty."

"I'll remember," Arn said.

THE MOON WAS LIKE A SILVER DOLLAR PITCHED ON A BLUE tablecloth, and moonlight goes a long way on the prairie. The bluestem was gone now, burned away by the drought; the naked land was flat and somehow cold in the blue-white light. Arn saw the buggy from a long way off, and dug his heels into the plug that still served him for transportation, coaxing him into a fat-back trot.

"She's gone out," the Reverend's wife had said, in a state of some alarm. "And, Henry, she took the buggy. She didn't even ask me, really; just said she was taking it."

And the Reverend had blinked and stuttered a little and wondered where a girl like Miss Larson could have gone by herself, in a buggy, at this hour of the night.

"I think I know," Arn had told them, and he'd been right.

She must have seen him approach, or at least heard the horse's feet in the incredible quiet, but she gave no sign. Arn pulled up and peered inside. She was leaning forward in the seat, her chin in her hand, looking toward the house at the end of the trail that cut off the road and went across the stubble.

"You're very foolish to come out here," he said sharply. "At night, and alone."

"I wanted to see it," she said. "The house that was never mine, and never will be. I wanted to see it before I left. How did you know where I was?"

"When you weren't at the preacher's, I figured it," Arn said. He dropped the lines over the plug's head and slid to the ground. Then, with exaggerated politeness, he took off his hat and knocked on the dashboard. "Anybody home?"

"Come on," she said, and he saw her smile. "If I'd have known you were coming, I'd have whipped up a cake—no, I wouldn't." The fooling faded from her voice. "I'd have driven on, somewhere. I didn't want to talk to anybody tonight, Arn."

He sat beside her.

"Weren't you going to tell me about going at all?"

"Tomorrow morning, on the way to the depot. Just before train time, so you wouldn't have much chance to argue with me." Her hand moved across the space between them and came to a stop on top of his own. "Don't argue with me now, Arn. I've made up my mind. Just sit here with me."

He took the hand in both of his, and for a while they sat unmoving, unspeaking. There seemed to be no tension in Mattie. She was calm, almost placid. But a storm grew in Arn; the silence smothered him; the silence was final and stifling, like dirt on the lid of a coffin. He had to talk. He had to move.

"Don't go," he burst out.

"You promised," she said.

"Don't go!"

With a sudden movement he pulled her toward him, pinning the arms that tried to push him away. She wore nothing on her head, and now he saw that her hair was loose. It flooded over her shoulders and down her back. When she turned her head away, he laid his mouth against her neck, underneath the ear.

"Arn—"

"All right, all right," he whispered. "Then let me kiss you once, just once. For good-by." He was lying; at this moment the thought of her going was impossible. But at this moment he would tell her anything. He was lying, and he thought she knew it. But her head came around and her mouth came up, half-open.

"Just once. . . ."

He kissed her, and for an instant she was limp in his arms. Then he felt her tighten and her fingers touch the back of his neck, and he knew that it would be more than once.

"I'm a straight-thinking woman," she said, when they finally talked again. "And I'd never even thought of our doing that until it happened, the other day. And now, since then—I've thought about nothing else." She closed her eyes. "Why didn't you kiss me a long time ago, Arn, a long, long time before—before anything else—"

"I thought about it. I guess I was afraid to ask."

"Do people have to ask?" she said, and when his head came down again she met him more than halfway.

"Then all this talk about leaving sounds a little silly. At least we've got that settled."

"It was settled before you touched me. I can't stay here. Maybe it sounds ridiculous and—and female, but I told you. If I stay, someday Luke will kill you. Not because of me, exactly; because of himself. This is a brutal place, and it does brutal things to people."

"You're going to stay here," Arn said in a fierce whisper. "For me. Why did you come back here tonight, except for our being here before? What did you feel when I kissed you? If you're a straight-thinking woman, Mattie, don't tell lies to yourself."

"You make it sound simple," she said. "But if you're right about my feelings—I'm not saying that you are, Arn, I won't say that—then you know why I have to go."

"No," he said, and bent over her again.

It was different this time. Without his knowing it, there had been a precipice, and now they were over it. She was loose in his arms, and she turned her head away the moment he released her. She looked across the prairie to the soddie. As he watched her face, wetness glinted in the corners of her eyes.

"Do you want to go inside?"

She pulled her breath in sharply and turned away.

"I mean—alone?" he said, almost harshly.

"No," she said. "Now I want to go back, and finish packing my things."

AT MIDNIGHT THAT SAME NIGHT DOCTOR HOMER CHUBB WAS summoned to his office to repair the damage to a railroad section hand who had attempted to dive from the top of the Pacific House, over in Joyville, into the establishment's watering trough and had broken his femur in the process. Doc not only splinted him up but also put three cups of scalding coffee down him. The gentleman was taken away by his friends, almost sober and terrified by his memories.

As Doc blew out his lamp and prepared to lock the office door behind him, he observed that the chambers of Ed Columbine were also lighted. There was a movement of feet inside and, as Chubb hesitated, Mr. Arthur Grossinger came out. He wheezed a good night in Doc's general direction and hurried down the steps, leaving the door open.

"Ed," Chubb called, "could we talk for a couple of minutes?"

"Come in, come in. You realize, of course, that my fee for consultation after midnight is double the ordinary."

Mr. Columbine had removed both his coat and his vest, and his sleeves were rolled up to the gaiters. It was hot in the room; a man working at night had the choice between closed windows or an invasion of night bugs, and Mr. Columbine preferred the heat. He mopped his face with a soggy handkerchief.

"Matter of fact, I wanted to talk to you, Homer. What the devil's come over you?" Mr. Columbine had an air of amiable curiosity. "Never saw you on the street before without that pretty pair of forty-fours, and then that ordinance thing—"

"I'm part Indian," Doc grinned. "I read signs. Look, Ed, this town's got to grow up. Neither one of us could stop it, even if we wanted to. Personally speaking, that means I've got to grow up, too. Maybe age fifty-five is a little late, but I finally made it."

"Lordamighty, Homer," the lawyer said scornfully, "this is a man's country, and it's going to stay that way. I thought you knew that as well as I do." He dug a cheroot from the elegant box. "Of course," he murmured, "everybody here loves your crotchety old soul, and you never had to use that fancy hardware. Maybe that makes a difference. By the way —what did you do with those guns?"

"Locked them in my desk. Why?"

"Well, the marshal is turning out to be a pretty good workman. I thought we might have some new butt plates made and make a little presentation. With the thanks of the City, all that."

"He's already asked me. I told him no. Same thing I'm telling you now." Doc crossed his short legs and smoothed

62

the unpressed fabric with his palm. "Ed, I want to fire Luke off that job, but if there's a fight about it, the Council will have to be on my side. That's why I came to talk to you."

Columbine's shaggy eyebrows went down in a thoughtful crease.

"Tonight you really got everything wrong end to, haven't you, Homer? We finally got a real man for marshal of this town, and now you want to fire him. What have you got against Luke?"

"I like him. I want him fired for his own sake. That boy is—is sick, in a funny kind of way. Have you ever noticed the way he touches a gun? The way another man would touch a woman. And after he's used a gun, he's all wound up, riding a high wave, like somebody who's just won the big foot race at the County Fair. I'll bet my last nickel that he doesn't sleep much any more."

"Hell, the job's a strain," Columbine said. "You're a doctor; you ought to understand that. He looks all right, doesn't he?"

"A lot of final-stage consumptives look all right, too," Doc grunted. "There's some other things. He's got this howling vanity, and now he's got an audience. When he walks down the street, he picks up a crowd that laughs when he laughs, gets tough when he gets tough, spits when he spits. Yesterday afternoon I saw a Mex kid I'll bet wasn't eighteen with a holster tied to his thigh and an old .38 stuck in it, walking soft and easy on his toes—imitating. Ed, when you add that kind of vanity to gun-craziness, you've got—"

"—A damn fine officer of the law."

"He happens to be on the side of the law, but it's an accident. One little push and he'll be on the other side. I don't want to see that happen."

Columbine got up, the cheroot clamped in the corner of his mouth.

"This is a big country," he said, "and, I repeat, it's for big men. If a man starts to shrink when he's fifty-five, it's too bad. For the man. Nothing doing, Homer. As long as I've got anything to say about it, Luke stays."

Then, with a brisk movement that changed the subject once and for all, he dug into his desk and came up with a handful of checks held together by an india-rubber band.

"Odd time of night for city business," he grinned, "but since you're here, we might as well get these signed."

Checks drawn on the city's account had to be signed by both the mayor and the city treasurer; Doc observed that Grossinger's signature was already on these. He took the pen which Columbine handed over.

"Just the usual things," the lawyer said. "Routine—What's that for?"

After he scratched his signature on the first one, Doc Chubb made a notation on the back of an envelope which had come from his pocket.

"I've signed a lot of checks without paying much attention to them," he said. "Almost without looking. Thought maybe I'd start to keep a record."

There was the briefest kind of silence before Mr. Columbine laughed.

"Why start now?"

"Oh . . . matter of principle. You're a lawyer, Ed. You'd know about principle."

AT EIGHT THIRTY THE NEXT MORNING ARN DROVE HER TO THE depot in Reverend Minner's buggy. At first Mattie objected to this, but when he assured her that he would be at the station whether she wanted him there or not, she gave in and let him take the lines.

Luke was at the depot, too. They tied the buggy across the street and walked over, Arn lugging a carpetbag in each hand, and when they came around the corner of the building onto the platform, Luke was there. Mattie flushed a little.

"Did you tell him about leaving?"

"I sent a note around last night."

"Not exactly the most honest way to do it, but the best, maybe."

"It'd be hard to face Luke."

She could have meant anything by that, and Arn found nothing in her face to help. He put the bags neatly against the wall, side by side.

"Well, you'd better get ready," he muttered. "Because you're going to have to face him now."

The morning train did not draw crowds as big as the evening arrivals, but there were still a substantial number of citizens about. Luke spoke to many of them as he came across the platform, touching his hat to the ladies and grinning the one-sided grin.

"Well, child!" he said, reaching for both of Mattie's hands. "I know you didn't want me to come, but I came down anyhow. If you'd rather I didn't stick around—"

"It's all right, Luke," she said.

"And the merchant prince," Luke said. "How's business, Arn?"

"Good enough." Arn was a little puzzled; after the brief touching of hands with Mattie, Luke had taken a couple of steps backward and stood three or four feet away. Maybe

64

that was why he spoke so clearly, almost loudly. Anybody within twenty feet could hear; there were several people within that distance.

"I'm sorry I didn't let you know before, Luke," Mattie whispered. "It was sort of a—sudden idea."

The petulant hoot of the KP engine cut the clear warmth of the morning.

"We both understand about that," Luke said. "And I'm glad it's your decision, not mine."

From the corner of his eye Arn saw Mr. Chambers, the undertaker, nudge his chubby wife with the traveling bag. Mr. Chambers winked. And then, for the first time, Arn realized what was going on.

He swung toward Mattie. Unconsciously, she was helping; with her empty face and the confused unhappiness of her eyes, she was the very picture of a rejected female.

"It had to be my decision," she said. "How could it have been anyone—"

Luke lifted his voice above the rattle of the approaching train.

"And I'm sorry," he said. The dark eyes were like pin points; they ate into the girl's face. "But a man can change a lot in almost a year." By this time there was a casual semicircle around them, frankly listening. "His feelings can change. But I'm honestly sorry, and I hope we'll still—"

Rage exploded in Arn's entrails like a flash of gunpowder.

"Luke," he said, "you're a liar."

He lunged for him. Luke's right hand made the automatic gesture and then hung, trembling, above the gun. The next moment Arn hit him. He hit him the way a man hits a door he is trying to crash, with his shoulder up and his head tucked down, awkwardly but with tremendous force. Luke went backward on the wooden planking of the platform with a crash, and his holster spilled. Arn caught the gun with the toe of his boot and sent it sliding. Luke came swiftly to his feet.

Neither of them made any attempt to dodge a blow; they stood with their boots almost touching and poured their strength blindly at each other. The fight was brutal, but as soundless as a faked battle in a play; the racket of the slowing locomotive swallowed all sounds of impact, of bone on bone. With triumphant surprise Arn realized that Luke did not have the edge in physical strength that he'd had even a month ago; Luke wasn't hitting as hard, and some of his swinging was wild. Arn bored in. A couple of punches found the softness above the gun belt.

The marshal would have gone down, except for the hand that caught his lawn shirt at the second stud. With cold precision Arn held him upright and threw the right with all his weight behind it. It was the last blow he was able to throw.

There was a movement behind him, but he was aware of it too late. Before he could let go and turn, the gun barrel crashed against the side of his head.

Mattie saw the gangling young man who wore a battered trooper's hat move into the fight. There was a badge on his vest, which meant that he was one of Luke's new deputies. She saw him swing the gun up and made a desperate attempt to catch his hand; at best, she only slowed the blow a little. Arn dropped almost at her feet.

Most of the passengers had descended from the train to watch, and there was an angry mutter against the deputy. The code about interference in other people's fights was strong in this country. She dropped beside Arn and, taking his head between her hands, examined the welt that was already rising.

"Get him up. Get him on his feet!"

She looked up. Luke stood over them, his feet spread, rocking a little. Blood came from the corner of his mouth, and his eyes were wild.

"He can't," she said. "He's out."

"Nobody finishes my fights for me; I finish them myself. Get him up!"

"If you rubbernecks have had enough of this," said a bored voice in the crowd, "I'd like to get this train moving again. *'Boooooooard!'*"

The movement back into the train started in a general mumble of disappointment.

"He's faking," Luke snarled. "He's afraid to get up."

"He's hurt, you fool!"

The train conductor herded the last of his customers aboard and then, with one foot on the step, turned back to glance at the platform.

"Anybody else going?" he said.

Mattie looked up, and the sweep of his eyes across the platform stopped as it reached her face. His brows went up inquiringly.

She shook her head, and bent over Arn again.

WHEN HE OPENED THE DOOR TO LEAVE DOC CHUBB'S OFFICE, the heat pushed by the prairie wind hit him like the blast from a furnace. He blinked and shook his head against the hard brilliance of the sunlight.

"I'll walk you down to the store," Mattie said. "You're a little shaky on your feet yet."

"I'll manage," Arn said. With the tips of his fingers he touched the bandage over his right ear. "Feels like I'm carrying a barrel on my shoulders, Doc."

"It'll come off in a few days, as soon as that laceration's closed over. Don't like to have a skin break in an area dirty as the hair."

"I know." Arn grinned feebly. "Germs."

Mattie followed him outside.

"I'd be glad to walk down to the store with you, Arn," she said. "I want to."

He ran his hand lightly down the length of her arm and gripped her fingers for a moment.

"No, Mattie."

He turned away from the hurt question in her eyes and headed for the street. After a few steps walking became an automatic process again and, despite the heat, he increased his speed. One thing was certain—the word about the fight had already gone around Railhead. Conversations had a way of stopping as he passed people on the street.

The store was dark and almost cool when he let himself in; the thick stone of the walls held what coolness came in the night. There were no customers waiting, and for this he was grateful. He went directly to the back of the store.

There was a short wooden rack at the end of the counter and fitted in it, muzzle down, were four revolvers. Expert recommendations to the contrary, this was his entire stock of personal weapons. He glanced down the rack and then, more or less at random, took the second one. It was an S & W .38 with dark-brown walnut handles. There was moisture in the palm of his hand as he lifted it.

He wore no holster, but he awkwardly made the motion anyhow—holding the gun against his hip and then lifting it and throwing the barrel. He did it a half-dozen times, a grim smile tight on his lips.

Luke had won, after all.

THIS WAS JULY, AND THE TRAIL HERDS FLOODED INTO RAIL-head like rivers into an arm of the sea. On the 8th a total of twenty-three thousand head was reached; there had been eleven thousand the day before. The stock pens of the KP held only the smallest fraction of such a tide; the rest of the sea of beef settled in an ever-growing pattern around the town, like waters backed up by a dam. The sound of an uncounted multitude of hooves, mixed with bawling and the whiplash yip of the hands, was so constant that the citizens of Railhead no longer heard it, as people who live on the shore cease to hear the surf. But they did hear the quiet at night, when the cattle bedded—and sometimes they stiffened in their beds when the rumble of movement came through the dark. Two or three times there had been the beginnings of a stampede; every time it had been brought under control and, besides, the panicky movement of the cattle was away from town. But a scared longhorn is not very particular about where he runs, and people joked that there was a longhorn for every blade of grass in the county.

The tangle down around the actual loading pens, west of Railhead's business district, was a twenty-four-hour nightmare. It was impossible to hear among the pens; men trying to make social pleasantries screamed at each other like hysterical girls. Standing on the roofed platform which overlooked the uproar, Arn Hendricks could feel the dust soaking into him like spray off a waterfall. He was looking for Mr. Arthur Grossinger, councilman and city treasurer of Railhead—and if Grossinger was down there somewhere, Arn half-hoped he wouldn't be able to find him.

Fortunately Mr. Grossinger was also on the platform, although it took Hendricks a while to find him. He sat at the far edge with his feet over the side, by himself, his back toward the pens. It was the heavy movement of his breath, lifting his shoulders, that finally identified him. Arn dropped beside him.

"If you're busy, it can wait," he said, lifting his voice above the racket. "But I thought maybe we could have that talk now."

"About what?"

"Columbine said the other night that you'd explain about the city financial setup."

"You mean you—you actually want me to?" Mr. Grossinger's breathing became more painful.

"Why not?"

"Well—no reason, exactly, but nobody else ever did—"

Arn had never actually looked closely at the man before, and he revised downward his first impression of Grossinger's age. He was not middle-aged; early forties, maybe, but sickness had marked his face with the echoes of pain, and the hair that showed beneath his grimy hat was grey. Once he had been well-built; the shoulders beneath the frowzy coat were broad but limp. Grossinger had the look of a man who had been kicked in the stomach a lot of times and now, in patient fear, awaits the next one.

"Then it's high time," Arn grinned.

The cattle trader's mouth opened and then closed again. He shrugged and let himself down to the ground.

"The stuff is up in my office," he said, nodding at the frame building that sat a couple of rods back of the platform. This overgrown shack, which had never been painted, was actually one of the most important structures in Railhead. The business doings of the cattle trade were centered here, in narrow and naked rooms under roofs that let the rain in. Half-joking, the people of Railhead called it the Exchange.

"The way I see it," Arn said as they walked, "running a town is just like any other business, but more important than most—because there are a lot more stockholders."

"Well—" Grossinger said. "Well, yes. Yes, I guess you could say that."

He pulled in a long breath and let it out again with a rattle.

Grossinger's quarters were on the second floor, reached by means of an outside stairway. Arn could have covered the length of the room with three strides, the width with two. There was a deal table with a clutter of papers on it, a couple of small wooden boxes containing more papers, and two chairs. Arn noticed the bedroll in the corner. Grossinger apparently slept here, which was not surprising; a good bed was one of the rarest—and most expensive—things in Railhead, particularly during this time of year. But the bedroll didn't go with the picture on the table. The brown print was of a handsome young woman and a man who stood behind her, clutching the back of the chair. Arn looked inquiringly at the man beside him, the ghost of the man in the photograph.

"My wife," he said. "She was my wife. She died of the Asiatic cholera. We came down here from Iowa for my health." His mouth twisted bitterly. "A great joke, eh?"

"I'm sorry."

"I'm not," the cattle trader said. "Considering." Then, with an abrupt gesture, he started pawing into the papers. "We've got books, but they aren't here. Sent them to Kansas City for audit."

He spoke from the pile of papers, without looking up.

"When do you expect them back?"

"Oh . . . couple, three weeks. It takes a while."

"Then you must have some kind of working books, some kind of record for the meantime."

"There's some stuff here. Ed has some of it over at his place."

69

"Columbine?"

"He helps me some. Ed's handy with figures."

"I'll bet," Hendricks said drily. "But you're the city treasurer."

Grossinger looked at him sharply.

"Hendricks, are you accusing me of negligence?"

"I'm not accusing anybody of anything. Dammit, man, I have to do with the government of this town, and I'd like to know a little about it."

The cattle trader reached out to the far side of the table for a folded sheet, and as his coat fell open, Arn noticed the little parlor pistol in a holster fastened to the lining.

"There's this," Grossinger said. "For the six months ending June first."

It was simply a balance sheet, and a balance sheet can be meaningless, but it was better than nothing at all. Arn dropped into the other chair, awkwardly shifting the holster on his hip so that it rode more comfortably, and began to read.

It was an incredible document.

"$3,217.25 for interest?" Arn said. "Interest on what?"

Grossinger wore a watch chain across his soiled vest, and a small gold nugget hung from the chain by a loop. He bounced the nugget with his finger tips.

"Bonds. Bonded—indebtedness."

"For what?"

The nugget bounced faster.

"Sidewalks and street."

Arn blinked at him.

"Are you joking? I'd bet my left eye that this so-called interest alone is more than has been spent on sidewalks and streets since this town was built. . . . Eight hundred fifteen dollars and fifty cents for wood, oil and et cetera. What's et cetera?"

"That would be in the books, and I told you the books—"

"Are in Kansas City; I know." Arn sighed. "Well, suppose we take a look at the credit side. Total receipts for fines, December first to June first. Nine hundred eleven dollars and seventy-five cents. I'd say that was about right for one month, not six."

Grossinger had the watch chain twisted in a hard knot around his fingers, and his lips worked noiselessly against each other. Arn found it hard to look at him.

"This thing is just plain childish," he said, tossing the balance sheet back to the table.

"You'd do me a favor if you'd get the hell out of here," Grossinger said thickly. His breath came hard.

"There's a couple of things I'd like to ask about first. Un-

70

derstand you and Doc Chubb both sign the checks for official disbursement. Do you have a record of those—how many, and how much? Do you sign in each ot'ier's presence, at some kind of official meeting, or—"

Grossinger's hand came down on the table with a crash.

"When the books are back, I'll talk to you," he said, coming to his feet. "In the meantime, you'd better be real careful about jumping to any conclusions. You could get in trouble."

"What's the name of this auditing outfit in Kansas City where you sent the books?"

"I don't remember; I'd have to look it up. Get out."

Arn got slowly to his feet and, reaching behind him, opened the door.

"Mr. Grossinger," he said quietly, "are there any books, or do you and Ed Columbine just carry everything . . . in your heads?"

The cattle trader clawed at his watch chain. It snapped between his fingers.

"Are you calling me a liar?"

"I wouldn't do that until I was sure, and I'm not. But there's one thing I'm sure about. You're scared. I intend to find out about the books, but I also intend to find out what you're scared of."

He closed the door quietly and went out, and the sound of Grossinger's tortured breathing followed him down the hall.

THAT DAY HE SPOKE WITH MATTIE FOR THE FIRST TIME SINCE the fight with Luke on the station platform, three days before. He had seen her half a dozen times, coming and going past the store, but neither of them had made any real attempt to come together. Arn had avoided it; somewhere in the back of his mind was the idea that the inevitable conversation would go easier if someone else started it.

But on Friday evening, after he had padlocked the hardware business and taken his dinner alone in the dining room of the Cattleman's Rest, he paid a call to the home of the Reverend Henry Minner and asked if Miss Larson would be so good as to descend to the parlor. Mrs. Minner went upstairs with the summons, and the Reverend, with an apologetic smile, reminded him of one of the house rules.

"Not in the parsonage, if you please," he said, pointing with a lean forefinger. "You can put it on the taboret, at the door."

For a moment Arn failed to realize what he was talking about. Then, with a stammer of apology, he hastily unhitched the gun belt and carried it to the spot Minner had indicated.

71

When he turned around, Mattie stood at the back of the room, watching him.

With a discreet cough, the Reverend made his way out. Arn and the girl looked at each other in silence.

"I'd heard about that," she said finally, indicating the gun. "Everybody in town has talked about it. Most people seem to be a little disappointed that neither of you has shot the other yet."

"I'm not planning on any shooting, and I hope it never comes," Arn said. "But—I had to, Mattie. After the other day, there was nothing else to do."

"Why not?"

"Because I gave Luke a licking, and Luke being what he is, he'll have to try to make it up. I hope that can happen without anybody touching a trigger, but—"

"I didn't ask you to go after him," she said. "You weren't obliged to defend what I guess you thought was my honor."

"You know that you'd never been willing to have me if I'd done anything else."

The shadow of a bitter smile touched her lips.

"Am I supposed to want you, Arn?"

"Why else did you stay?"

"There could be woman reasons, you know. If I'd taken that train and gone away, it would have seemed to those snickering loafers that Luke was right, wouldn't it?—that I left with a broken heart, a castoff woman. Maybe I'm staying to face them down."

"Maybe," Arn said. "Maybe we don't need to worry about the reasons."

He took her by the shoulders.

"I don't give a damn why you stayed," he said harshly. "I want you, Mattie, and I'm going to do everything in my power to get you. Make up your mind to it."

She pulled herself free and turned away. He could not see her face, and she said nothing, but he made no attempt to touch her again. Mrs. Minner's moonfaced wall clock sighed and struck eight brassy, businesslike strokes.

"Meanwhile," Arn went on, with a sudden lightness, "you are a beautiful and unattached young woman. With a bunch of snickering loafers to face down. In that connection, I came to ask you to the theater."

"The what?" she said.

"The play, lady. I remember how you liked it back home, back where the trees grow. There's a traveling troupe tomorrow night."

"Who?"

"A Mr. Chichester. I never heard of him, but the program

includes monologues, a hilarious Farce entitled *Shakespeare Undone*, a tableau of beautiful young women representing the Four Seasons, with music, and—in conclusion—two soliloquies from *Hamlet.*"

"*Shakespeare Undone*," she said. "I wonder what that's like?"

"I don't know," Arn said. "But I saw Mr. Chichester when he was tacking up his posters today, and if anybody's going to undo Shakespeare, he's just the man."

MR. ALLERDYCE CHICHESTER AND COMPANY PRESENTED THEIR performance in the Grand Salon of the Cattleman's Rest, a room some thirty by fifty feet which served as the arena for visting pugilists, public dances, lectures on a variety of subjects by men invariably titled Professor, and occasional sermons by itinerant ministers of the gospel. Mr. Chichester later expressed pain at the wounding of his artistic pride by the events of the evening. He did not mind having to evict an occasional drunken cowhand from the stage, he said, but these dislocations of the audience were far too common in Kansas towns. Mr. Chichester's complaint had some justification, for he and a charming young woman he introduced as his niece had hardly finished the Introductory Song when the robbery of the paymaster for the Kansas Pacific railroad took place and all hell broke loose.

The holdup was simple both in plan and execution. Every Saturday night a man from the division paymaster's office arrived in Railhead on the westbound train with cash for the payment of wages. The amount varied, but it was generally between eight and ten thousand dollars. The messenger traveled in the mail car and was escorted across the platform and into the ticket office by two armed guards. He then installed himself at one of the two windows with the local payroll; a line was established outside, on the platform, and the men were paid off one at a time. Section gangs and building crews were a rather vigorous lot, particularly on a Saturday night, and for this reason only two or three men were admitted to the building at one time.

There was always a lag of perhaps a quarter hour after the time the building was closed to public business and before the pay-off started while the money was sorted and the payroll set up. It was during this time that the gunmen struck.

It was later determined that they must have been on the premises at the time the train arrived; when the building was emptied they hid themselves in the express office, after binding and gagging the man stationed there. While the pay mes-

73

senger was a.ranging his currency in convenient piles, they simply appeared before the window with drawn guns. There were three of them. They were not masked.

At this time there was one guard inside the office, along with the messenger, the stationmaster, and the telegrapher. The guard had a shotgun, and he made the mistake of trying to use it. He was blown apart by a double-barrel looped around the neck of the tallest of the three. In the general shooting that followed, the messenger was also killed and the stationmaster and telegrapher wounded. One of the holdup men was hit, but he got away with the others, after most of the money had been scooped into a leather sack. They made their escape across the tracks into Joyville and rode off on horses that had been tethered behind a canvas tent that housed a twenty-four-hour-a-day crap game.

While this was going on, Marshal Luke Malette was in the lobby of the Cattleman's Rest, preparing to buy a ticket to the performance of Mr. Chichester and company. He was summoned immediately, as was Doctor Chubb, and made a brief investigation. He then returned to the hall, where most of the regular citizens of Railhead were absorbing culture, to raise a posse.

Arn had heard the distant clatter of gunfire, as had everybody else, but such a noise was not unheard of in Joyville on a Saturday. He saw Mattie make a face at the noise, but she said nothing and joined with enthusiasm the applause at the end of the Introductory Song.

Mr. Chichester had just reappeared on-stage, in blackface and carrying a gunny sack which presumably contained a stolen chicken, when Luke came down the aisle between the improvised seats. He vaulted to the platform and spoke briefly to the actor, who threw his arms toward heaven in appeal and then withdrew.

"I need some men," Luke said. It struck Arn that, oddly, Luke was not out of place up there; the grace of his movement, the elegance of his clothes in the colored light were somehow more dramatic than Mr. Chichester's best efforts. Maybe Luke knew it, too; he wasn't intimidated by the situation.

"There's been a shooting at the depot over the KP payroll," he said. "Couple men dead, and they made off with most of the money. Let's get on that trail."

The room was in an uproar almost immediately, and there was a general movement toward the door.

"Wait a minute!" Luke called sharply. "I don't want a ragtag mob riding all over the prairie. I don't know how long we'll be out; I suspect those boys have headed for Texas. I want five or six at the most"—a forest of hands went up— "and I'll do my own picking."

His eyes flickered over the crowd.

"Harris—Primrose—you too, Wagonwheel—" He ticked them off rapidly, pointing at each one. Most of them had some reputation as handy men with a gun; one, Cy Flaherty, had been an Indian scout and could follow signs. The marshal hesitated for a moment after he named the fourth one. A trace of the crooked grin came to his face.

"And Mister Hendricks," he said, sighting down the outstretched hand with its pointing finger. An instant silence touched the room, and heads came around.

"Stand up, gentlemen!" Luke said. Boots banged against the planking. "So far as I'm concerned, you're sworn in. You're all deputies. We'll organize at the depot in twenty minutes and if you can bring an extra horse, so much the better."

They broke for the door, but for a moment Arn didn't move. All the way down the length of the room he could see the mocking light in Luke's dark eyes.

He turned to Mattie.

"You see the rest of it and then get somebody to take you home," he said. "Don't go home alone."

He clapped on his hat and hurried after the others.

EVEN IN THE DARK OF THE MOON, THE PRAIRIE IS NEVER COMpletely dark. In the summer the clear night sky is a dark crystal-blue, and like crystal it seems to have within it a light of its own. It is possible to see a man on horseback for a long way on such a night, especially if his mount is spotted or if he wears white.

There was not enough light to track, however, even if any distinguishable sign had shown in the sunburnt stubble. The gunmen were seen heading south, along the cattle trail, and this was the route that the posse took. They rode at a steady trot.

Arn had not been able to get an extra horse; he was lucky to have one as it was, since he'd had to borrow. The faithful plow pony was not up to posse work by a long way. Arn had run into Ralph Coleman, editor of the Railhead *Observer*, outside the door of the Paris Girl Saloon. Editor Coleman weighed two hundred and forty pounds and on this particular Saturday night there was gin in every ounce. He had been amiable to the notion of lending his fine roan; he had even insisted.

They forded the Dead Indian River at the cattle ford; the

75

soddie that Luke and Arn had built was to the west, almost within sight, but if either of them noticed it they made no sign. Luke had not spoken directly to him since they left. They splattered through the trickle of water that had been left by the July sun without slackening their pace and drove deeper south.

Arn was not a horseman, not in the cattleman's sense, and even the rocking-chair gait of the roan began to pound him after a while. His legs grew heavy and senseless; from time to time he pulled his feet from the stirrups, one foot at a time, and swung them back and forth to get the blood moving again. The dust ate into his lungs, even after he tied a handkerchief across the lower part of his face, and the holster that held the new .38 banged against his leg at every stride.

About two in the morning they circled a bedded trail herd and Luke rode over to check with the hands. It was the first break in five hours, and when Arn slid gratefully from the saddle his heels banged the ground so hard that his bones rattled. He took a few careful steps on legs that seemed to have no connection with his body.

"That marshal," Wagonwheel said, "is one helluva hard-drivin' man."

Wagonwheel—nobody knew his other name, if he had one —had been a hunter for the KP before he became a built-in fixture of Joyville's saloons, and his old buffalo gun was holstered to his saddle.

"Drivin' right into a rainstorm, I'd guess," Cy Flaherty muttered. "If it rains, we're sure to lose them. This whole thing's kind of half-cocked anyhow; how does he know they didn't swing east? They might be heading square for Kansas City right now."

Arn tilted his head back and looked at the sky. He was not as conscious of plains weather as the men who had spent their lives here, and he hadn't noticed the cloud bank crawling in from the northwest. It was an even black line, like the stroke of a brush in an invisible hand, and as he watched he thought he could see it move, swallowing the stars, dulling the crystal.

"Thank God," he said. "We need it."

"We don't need it when we're in the middle of it," Flaherty growled. "Maybe you're waterproof, but I ain't."

The smallest sparks of lightning were touching the horizon when Luke came back.

"Let's go," he said. "We're headed right; one of the men on the picket saw three riders circle past about an hour ago. That would be Mr. McCloy and his friends."

"McCloy?" Arn said.

"Didn't you know?" Luke laughed; a quick, dry sound.

"The telegrapher had seen that ruckus at the box supper. Besides, who else do you know that wears a shotgun around his neck?"

"It's going to rain like all the slop pails of Hell," Flaherty said. "When we go two months without water and then it comes, we always get too much."

"I don't see any rain," Luke said.

Flaherty pointed with a bony finger.

"Chappie, that's still in Wyoming," Luke said. "Let's ride."

EITHER WYOMING WAS A LOT CLOSER THAN ARN THOUGHT OR else the wind that pushed the cloudburst was greased, because it was on top of them in less than three hours. There was a fantastic battle in the sky overhead; daylight rose in the east, and a darkness like midnight came from the west, and the posse rode for a while in a new world in between. For a few moments the reflected light of the sun, still below the horizon, splashed on the advancing breastworks of the clouds and turned them dirty yellow. The thunderhead in motion was a terrifying thing to see; it was so thick there was no seeing the top of it; its edges ' urled and whirled and burgeoned, and there was blue-white .ame in its belly.

Then the dirty ' low of the sun faded, and the dark waves rolled out and ' uched the eastern skyline, and it was dark again, except ior the lightning.

"I tell you we better get cover!" Flaherty shouted, when he found enough of a break in the roar of thunder to make himself heard. "She's going to blow right open."

Luke cursed with bitter fervor, but he reined up his gelding. The lightning broke again and the world was instantly white with blue shadows. For the first time Arn noticed the two buildings off a few hundred yards to their right. Luke jerked his mount around; his mouth moved, but he was soundless against the thunder. They went at a gallop.

This was some granger's place, from the looks of it; more ambitious than most, he had even started a barn. The framework was up, but the siding had gone only halfway, and there was no roof. Seen by lightning, the place looked deserted, which was not unlikely. The summer drought had burnt out a lot of homesteaders.

The trap into which the posse fell was a very obvious thing; if the ancient instinct to get out of nature's uproar hadn't pushed them so hard their approach would have been much more cautious.

As it was, they charged for the house at a gallop, thinking only of the storm.

They were already reining up, a bare fifteen yards away,

when the volley came from the house. The whipcrack of gunpowder was as trivial as a snap of the fingers in the racket of the storm. In bewilderment, Arn saw Wagonwheel's horse rear up and the rider fall backward, head over heels. Behind him, somebody yelled with pain. Then he caught the orange flash from the window and something hissed hotly past him, inches from his cheek. That time he knew what it was.

Then the rain came—at first, a handful of enormous drops. Flaherty and a couple of the others were already around, headed for the barn; one of them lay forward across the saddle horn. Arn jerked the roan in the same direction and beat his heels into its ribs, clawing for the .38 at the same time. Luke's gelding, riderless, trotted off a few paces and stood. Arn looked around frantically. Behind Wagonwheel's downed horse, using the belly for cover, was the marshal. He had a gun in each hand, and both of them were talking.

A bullet nipped the ground between Hendricks' feet as he slid off and dived for Luke's side. The rain was coming harder now. Cocking and pulling as fast as he could, Arn emptied the chamber in the general direction of the window where he had seen the last flash. Then, beside him, Luke let out a shout and lunged to his feet. A vague cluster of shapes detached from the other side of the house and moved away, and in an instant the curtain of rain had blotted them out.

Luke leaped over the body of the dead horse and started running toward his own mount. After three steps he was out of sight; with a final roar, the rain hit its climax and became a solid wall of water. Arn stopped trying to reload the revolver and put his head against the stomach of Wagonwheel's horse and made himself as small as possible. It was like being at the bottom of Niagara; the hammering literally nailed him to the ground.

He had no idea how long he stayed there, cowering and blind. It seemed an hour; it was perhaps five minutes. The whole face of the earth was awash. He had to lift his head to get his nostrils above the level of the water that stood on the prairie. When the first slackening came, when he could once again see the outline of the house, he got to his feet, and made for shelter. His boot toe snagged something. He recovered his footing and looked down.

Wagonwheel lay on his face, his legs pulled up under him and his arms flung wide. Blindly, instinctively, Arn hooked his hands under the hunter's armpits and tried to haul him upright. He got him only halfway when the weight slid from his wet grasp; he grabbed again.

But—face down.

He turned him over. The slug had gone in just behind his eye and come out above the ear on the other side.

Arn Hendricks straightened up and, with both hands cupped over his eyes to protect them against the drive of the rain, made his way to the house.

MR. MCCLOY AND COMPANY HAD APPARENTLY PLANNED TO catch up on a few of life's necessities in the deserted shanty. There was still a trace of heat from the fire which had been built, and an open bedroll was in the corner. Apparently they had figured on breakfast and a couple of hours' sleep, but the storm had driven the posse right into their laps. In a way, it had been lucky for the marshal and his boys; without the storm, they might have ridden past. But it hadn't been lucky for Wagonwheel.

Or for Lars Graves, who had a bullet through his ankle and a bootful of blood. Or for Nat Harris, one of Luke's regular deputies, who had a welt along his skull where a slug had creased him before ripping his ear and who still didn't make much sense when he tried to talk.

Cy Flaherty had managed to drag these two into the house a few minutes after Arn made it. Fortunately one corner of the place was comparatively dry, where the roof still held, and it was near enough to the window so they had a little light to examine the injuries. Arn and Flaherty hacked at the bedroll McCloy's boys had left behind, trying to fashion clumsy bandages.

Luke Malette had been the first one into the house; had been there when Arn arrived.

"It was raining so hard that I couldn't even find my horse." He had said it a dozen times by now. "I saw them pull out, but just as I tried to find my horse, whoosh!"

He spoke hoarsely, loudly, to make himself heard above the clatter of the rain. He walked to the wall and back again.

"Sit down, dammit," said Graves weakly from the floor, "before you step on somebody."

Nobody had to tell Arn Hendricks to sit down. He helped Flaherty wrap Graves's foot with a piece of the bedroll and then dropped into a corner. He did not sit; he dropped.

Luke moved to the window and stared out at the sheet of shimmering grey water. He smacked his fist against the sill.

"We can't sit here forever," he said. "Judas, this downpour could go on for days."

"Not at this rate," Flaherty said. "It'll quit by noon. Want to bet?"

"They can't travel far." If Luke heard him at all, he didn't indicate it. "That's what eats most—the thought that they're out there someplace, waiting it out—maybe within gunshot!"

79

Flaherty snorted.

"The seat of your britches is really afire, ain't it? What for? So maybe you don't get them; who cares?"

"I care! And I'll get them. I don't like the way you talk, Flaherty."

With a curious sense of detachment Arn became aware that this conversation and the people making it were drifting away from him. As if he were lying on the bank of a river and heard talk from a boat drifting by. Lying on the bank of a river; it was a nice thought. His eyelids dropped. Already they were out of sight, and the murmur of their voices faded.

With a deep sigh of pure pleasure, Arn Hendricks went to sleep.

Luke woke him up by kicking the soles of his boots. It was not a pleasant way to be awakened; the jarring pain went all the way to his shoulders. Even so, it was a long way back from the riverbank. When he finally opened his eyes, Luke was grinning at him.

"Sorry to be rough, chappie. But we've got riding to do."

The thought of mounting a horse again sent a pain through him that was worse than having his boot soles kicked. He leaned back against the wall for a moment. There was still rain, but it had diminished considerably.

"It's ten o'clock," Luke said. "Are you coming, or does the hardware business need you?"

Arn got up. Bending his legs was like touching himself with a hot iron, but one of the things that drove him up was the thought that Luke must be feeling much the same way. Luke hadn't exactly been born to the saddle either.

"Where are the others?"

"Flaherty is herding them into town, to the Doc. I suppose they needed it. And it suited Flaherty fine. He's got the soul of a puppy dog."

"You get the horses together?"

"Saddled already. They made it to the barn, which proves, I guess, that even a horse has sense enough to come in out of the rain."

But not some people, Arn said, but he said it to himself. He strapped the gun belt around his waist—the leather was stiff to his fingers and stinking to the nose—and reloaded the .38.

"So it's just the two of us," he said.

"That's right, chappie. It shouldn't be tough; there's just three of them. When I consider what a handy man you are with a gun, we practically outnumber them." The touch of mockery in Luke's voice was like vinegar. "The two of us. You might almost say it was like old times."

The rain beat upon them with a chilly dullness, as if it rained from a sense of duty, when they forked the saddles.

THEY HAD RIDDEN SOUTH NO MORE THAN A QUARTER OF A mile when they saw the hickory grove, a pathetic cluster of perhaps twenty trees left by afterthought on the vast flatness of the prairie. The rain still cut a man's vision in half, and they were almost upon it before they noticed. Luke rose in his stirrups.

"Like I said, almost within gunshot!"

They approached with a good deal more caution this time, making a full circle before they headed in, but there was no ambush. There was nothing but the unmistakable marks of hooves and boot heels and the droppings of the horses.

There was also a trail. In another thirty-six hours the top-soil of the prairie would be as hard as rock again; the stubble of the heat-burnt bluestem was so thick that, even now, the earth looked solid. But at the roots there was a layer of slip-pery goo that lifted with a horse's feet when he moved. A man with one eye could have trailed a rabbit on the stuff, and the three horses of McCloy's party left a swath like a troop of cavalry.

The trail did not continue south. It came out of the grove at right angles to the way it came in, almost straight west.

"It has to be them," Luke said. "Nothing else has been moving in this. They're circling back; they started south to make us think they were headed for Indian Territory, and then circled. McCloy talked about this new town, off to the west—"

"Dodge City," Arn said.

"Dodge, or the Colorado border—or, hell, right back where they came from."

"Maybe." Arn smiled wryly. "It would be quite a thing, wouldn't it, if they beat us back to Railhead."

"They aren't going to beat us anywhere," Luke said. "We can't be more than an hour or two behind."

The one-sided smile flickered on his face, and his shoulders moved with hard breathing, and he looked as if fatigue or pain had never touched him.

"Come on, chappie," he said softly.

They could move no faster than a good trot. The footing was slippery enough to give the horses trouble, and a horse with a broken leg would be fatal to the pursuit. Arn had a vague notion that the gait would have been punishing, if he'd been able to feel anything in his body any more. But the machinery that existed below his shoulders, that filled the saddle and fitted the stirrups and held the reins, was either dead or belonged to someone else.

"Just the two of us," Luke said. "Did you stop to think that it might be dangerous for you?"

He could have been talking about the time when they caught up with McCloy, but Arn knew that he wasn't.

"Why?"

"You know what people say. Everybody says I've got a score to settle, that I'm gunning for you; they expect it, now that you're carrying iron." He looked at him from the corner of his eye. "It would be easy, wouldn't it, Arn? Supposing now, right now, that I said *draw!* when I counted three. It'd be like fish in a barrel, wouldn't it?"

"Unless I drew when you got to 'two,'" Arn said grimly.

"That's right; I'd have to look out for that. After all, you're a businessman."

"What have you got against a man in trade, Luke? The same thing you've got against the sodbusters that are trying to make the prairie blossom? The same thing you've got against anybody who seems to want to make Railhead a town instead of a shooting gallery?"

There was no answer.

"It doesn't leave many people for you to like, does it? You can't very well like another man who packs a gun and intends to use it, because he may use it on you someday."

"I don't need anybody to like," Malette said fiercely. "I'm alone. I walk the streets alone and I ride alone; in the Paris Girl on a Saturday night I'm alone. That's the way I want it."

"But you need other people; if not for liking, for something else. One of the things that ate on you when we had the claim was the fact that it was lonesome. You need other people to cheer when you're the hero, laugh when you're funny, to be afraid when you're tough."

There was no anger in Arn's voice, but neither was there sorrow. He spoke as if he were reading an inventory.

"And, of course, you need—targets."

Luke stiffened in the saddle, and Arn half expected to see the right hand reaching; he braced himself. But Luke didn't go for the gun. His mouth twisted into a leer.

"You thought I was going to draw, didn't you, chappie? Don't worry. It's more interesting when it's close, and with you it wouldn't be. I brought you out here to see if you're a man."

"Got an answer yet?"

"I knew the answer before we came. I guess I'm just out to prove it now."

They rode the next half hour without speaking, in a rain that grew tired and got ready to quit. There was even a touch of yellow overhead, and Arn's soaked and shapeless clothes began to squirm against his skin. There was mud, a solid layer of it, over the lower half of his body; his boots were indistinguishable from the stirrups. His head ached, and the weight of his hat seemed intolerable. He pulled it off and beat as much water as possible out on the saddle horn.

Neither he nor Luke knew this part of the country, except in the vaguest kind of way; it was Kansas, flat and naked and limitless. They kept their eyes on the muddy swath cut by the horses of McCloy and his men and rode without looking at the horizon.

Therefore the creek was a surprise. They heard it long before they reached it; the roar was like a cataract. The land rose for several hundred yards, toward the little stand of scrub cottonwoods that squatted on what normally was the bank. Their trunks were deep in water now. Arn sucked in his breath when he got a good look at the water.

Yesterday a man probably could have stepped over this creek, or jumped it on the run. By tomorrow he might be able to do it again, but now it was a hundred feet wide and running at maniacal speed. The water was a muddy brown, with skiffs of unclean yellow foam touching the crests. It was filled with debris. The body of a young deer shot past; right behind it was the trunk of a dead cottonwood, as big around as a man's waist. When the log hesitated against some obstruction for a moment, the rush of water picked it up and flung it impatiently ahead, end over end.

The trail of the three riders led right to the edge.

Arn turned and saw Luke's mocking eyes upon his face.

"Maybe you'd better go first," Luke said, shouting to make himself heard above the uproar. "Then if you fall in, chappie, I can pull you out."

"Nobody could tackle that!"

"*They* did," Luke said indicating the track of the Texans.

"But that was an hour ago. Look at it; you can practically see it rise! Good God—"

"Like I said: I already know the answer. Now I'm just proving it."

"If you want to argue about who's a man, get off that horse and we'll settle it, any way you like. But I'm not going into that. It'll be passable in another three or four hours—"

He had no way of knowing how much Luke heard, or wanted to hear, because suddenly he threw back his head and laughed. The dark eyes hung with joyful relish on Arn's strained face. His laugh was a high whoop against the roar of water. Then it died, and with a contemptuous shrug Luke

83

socked his spurs into the sides of the gelding and drove him forward.

"Luke!"

The horse was spooky; he advanced slowly, trembling as he moved into the line of cottonwoods and the flood moved up to his belly. The water was still relatively quiet here, where the bank had been; the gelding plowed ahead until he crossed the line of the trees. Then he stopped cold.

"For God's sake, Luke!"

The shout was wasted in that racket. Luke pulled the hat from his head and beat his mount across the neck with brutal, flailing blows. The gelding screamed and roared and then plunged forward into the main channel.

He never even got his head up. For a crazy instant Luke Malette seemed to be sitting on top of the water, his hat still clutched in his hand, his mouth open in a wild shout. Then he pitched sideways and went in. For a few seconds Arn saw disconnected glimpses—a boot, an arm, a head—as if fragments of a man were awash in the flood. Then he saw nothing at all.

He sat motionless for maybe a full minute, staring at the spot where horse and rider had gone under. A desperate urgency boiled inside his stomach but could not move him. The water curled and twisted and howled beneath his eyes. Finally he lifted his head and shook it clear.

Then he nudged the roan frantically and rode downstream at the water's edge. The cream-colored hat had been caught against the root of a tree; the water worked it back toward the channel, patiently and slowly, and then caught it and flung it ahead, as if the parade had gone on and haste was necessary to catch up.

"Luke, Luke, Luke!"

He rode at a wild gallop, standing in the stirrups, racing the water, until the trembling horse beneath him slid to a stop from exhaustion. He made no attempt to push it further. Instead he let himself down and stood at the water's edge, screaming, a man gone crazy over the sound of one word:

"Luke—Luke—"

MR. EDWARD COLUMBINE, ATTORNEY-AT-LAW, LIFTED THE LID of the ormolu box and got himself a cheroot. He did not offer one to Mr. Grossinger, whose affliction kept him from smoking. As a matter of fact, any smoke at all in a room as small as the lawyer's office would make Grossinger uncomfortable. Mr. Columbine applied a match to the end of the cheroot and inhaled with deep satisfaction.

Mr. Columbine should have been in excellent spirits. It was a lot cooler after the day's rainfall; the hour was late, approaching midnight, and the late hours always filed the cutting edges of his mind to their keenest edge; his stomach was still comfortably full from an excellent dinner. Life was good, except for Grossinger.

"Judas Priest, man, you mean you showed him that balance sheet?"

"You made it up yourself." The cattle trader wheezed heavily and touched a handkerchief to his lips. "And, confound it, Ed, you even suggested that if he'd come see me I'd 'explain' about the city's money. Don't blame me."

"I didn't think he'd bother. And I thought you were smart enough, if he did, to palaver around him."

"He's not a fool. And you've dealt with fools—or at least with people who are too foolish to care—for so long you think you can get by with anything."

Mr. Columbine pawed a hank of hair out of his eyes and smiled around the cigar.

"Me? I'm not trying to get by with anything. You're the city treasurer; you're handling the public money."

"And don't jolly yourself into thinking he's foolish enough to go for that, either. He's looking deeper, Ed."

"This calling me by my first name is a new habit, Grossinger. I don't think I like it." Columbine plumed smoke at the ceiling. "I suppose you indicated that he should look deeper?"

"I did not!"

The lawyer shook his head with an air of weary regret.

"You've bobbled it," he said. "Too bad. I thought you were brighter."

Grossinger threw the handkerchief on the desk and his sick-shadowed eyes nailed into Columbine's.

"I'm plenty bright," he said. "Don't forget it. You'd never think of this, but—it hurt to have to mumble like an idiot to Hendricks, to see the contempt for my business sense in his eyes. By heaven, I'm a good businessman, and I can keep a straighter set of books than that whippersnapper ever dreamed of." His breathing was hard and tortured, and his eyes ran water. "I could have done fine things for this town, if—"

"You're a sick man, Grossinger," Columbine said. "Sick and stupid. You better go home and lie down."

"Be careful how you talk to me, lawyer. I get tired of fighting your battles by myself."

"Go home," Columbine said, completely bored.

Grossinger got to his feet, and if the lawyer had looked

closely he might have noticed that he stood taller than before.

"Hell, why should I fight your battle at all?" he said softly. "What have I got to lose?"

Columbine let him get to the door before he called after him.

"Grossinger," he said, "I hope you didn't mean that."

The cattle trader met his eyes for a moment and then, without speaking, turned and went outside, leaving the door open behind him.

Mr. Columbine smoked his cheroot all the way down before he moved from his chair. He was not a nervous thinker; when his mind chewed at a problem, it was not necessary for his feet to pace the floor or his body to contort itself. The only movement was that of his hand, to and from his mouth; there might as well have been a sign around his neck: MIND AT WORK. And when he finally ground out the cigar butt and stood up and reached for his hat, the book on Arthur Grossinger was closed.

He was ready to blow out the lamp when he heard the commotion on the stairs and the half grouchy, half gentle voice of Doc Chubb.

"I don't care what you think, we'd better have a good look," Doc growled.

"I'm tired, that's all." That was Hendricks' voice. "There's nothing the matter with me. I want a few hours' sleep and then I want to get out there again—"

"They don't need you. The search party's already organized."

Mr. Columbine moved out to the head of the stairs. Doc was half-carrying Arn Hendricks; he had one arm under the young man's shoulders and was hoisting himself along by gripping the rail with the other. The lawyer reached down and gave a hand.

Hendricks was a ghost. His face was drained of color, his eyes huge with fatigue. His clothes, starched with mud, had dried against his body like armor. They eased him into Chubb's office.

"Any luck?" Columbine asked, as Doc helped Arn out of his clothes.

"No."

There was a silence.

"I talked to Cy Flaherty when he came in with the wounded," Columbine went on. "Said you and the marshal were making it a two-man show."

Hendricks said nothing; he did not even look up.

"By the way—where is the marshal?"

He saw Doc stiffen, but for a long moment Hendricks

seemed to have heard nothing at all. Then his eyes flicked up and nailed squarely into the lawyer's.

"He's at the bottom of a creek out there. He was drowned when he tried to cross it during a flash flood. I don't even know the name of the creek."

"Yellowhair, probably," Chubb said. "Flaherty knows this country around here like the back of his hand, and he says, from the description, that it was probably Yellowhair."

"What happened?" Columbine said tautly.

"Just what I said. We were on McCloy's trail and we came to this creek, gone wild after that cloudburst, and Luke tried to ford it. He didn't have the chance of a rabbit, and I told him. Afterwards I looked for maybe an hour, but I couldn't find a trace of him."

"You got some fine bumps and bruises, but I guess you'll live," Doc grunted. He straightened up and looked at Columbine. "There's a search party headed out there now. They might find him, and he might be all right. You never can tell."

"I'll give bets at ten to one that they don't find a thing," Columbine said softly.

"What does that mean?" Hendricks said.

The lawyer shrugged.

"It just means that I'm a gambling man. Like any gambling man, I look the situation over and make a guess. You carry a gun now, don't you, Hendricks? And it's an open secret why you carry it. And a flood—well, a flood is a lot of water. Enough water to cover anything."

"Ed!" Doc Chubb blazed, whirling. "You shut—"

Hendricks had been sitting on the edge of the battered examination table, and it skittered across the room as he flung himself off it. Columbine side-stepped hurriedly. The wild punch dug into his shoulder and then Arn, unable to catch himself, catapulted past. The lawyer hit him sharply behind the ear. He crashed blindly into Chubb's desk and went down.

Columbine moved toward him, but a hand hooked his collar and jerked him backward.

"That's enough," Chubb grated. "If you want a fight, that's your business. But you don't come into my office and light into a patient. Get the hell out of here, Ed."

Columbine inspected the knuckles of his right hand and shook his head.

"I'm ashamed of myself, Homer," he said. "I haven't lifted a hand in a common brawl for years. It's hardly in keeping with the dignity of my profession. I apologize."

He pushed back his hair and tugged his vest straight and then, with another regretful shake of the head, let himself out without glancing again toward Hendricks. He stopped at the head of the stairs and went to check the door of his office to make sure it was locked. It was.

Then Mr. Columbine went down the stairs and into the street, whistling softly between his teeth.

SHORTLY BEFORE DARK THE NEXT DAY THE PARTY THAT HAD gone out to search for Luke Malette returned. They brought with them all that they had been able to find: a flat-topped hat, once cream-colored, now a mottled yellow and brown from river water. A few riders went out to meet them, and they picked up more followers as they came through town, both afoot and on horseback. By the time they reached the depot of the Kansas Pacific a considerable crowd had collected. It was an odd assembly; there was about it some of the flavor of a funeral cortege, as if the group had brought back a body instead of only a hat. This article passed through a good many hands, was identified by a dozen people— "That's his, all right, I'd know it anywhere"—each of them speaking as if only his opinion could make it certain.

There was another kind of talk, too. It concerned the fact that the marshal and Arnold Hendricks had been alone on the trail, and that there was only Hendricks' story of what happened, to go by. It lingered with delicate savor on the fact that these two gentlemen were known to have fought over a woman. Nobody said anything outright; when one young man tried to state his opinion in forceful language, lawyer Columbine (who had joined the circle) promptly hushed him by pointing out that any accusations were not fair play. Not until they had more to go on.

But, even without a public summing-up, almost everybody in Railhead was putting two and two together and arriving at the same four. It was the kind of story, rich with possibilities, that people like to believe, even the innocent and godly, even the people who didn't like the marshal. After the gathering at the depot broke up, the buzz-buzz went on; it expanded and grew like yeast in warm dough.

Seated in his room at the Cattleman's Rest, eating his dinner off the bureau, Arn Hendricks could hear none of this, but he knew about the talk. He could have repeated almost word for word what they were saying. It seemed to Arn that the notions that flew around Railhead came through the walls and floor and, bypassing his ears, were soaked up through his skin. He did not have much appetite.

He had slept until a little after noon. Doc Chubb had practically forced him into the hotel at the point of a gun, insisting that he spend at least one night—and preferably two—in a decent bed, even if there wasn't anything wrong with him. He was grateful to Doc now; the cushy feather tick of the hotel bed had felt like the lap of an angel. He reflected that it was about time he started looking for decent living quarters; the bedroll pitched in the back of the store was uncomfortably hard even before a day and night on horseback had jolted his bones loose.

Rufe Ford, one of the three bartenders downstairs, had brought him his supper, and now he came to fetch away the remains. Rufe had shoulders like a cattle car, and a constant smell of the barbershop about him.

"You finished, friend?"

Rufe smiled and his eyebrows curled in significant little arcs. Arn knew what Rufe was thinking, and he cared not a tinker's damn.

"Finished."

"You left a lot. What's the matter?" Rufe said.

"The smell of hair pomade always makes me sick at my stomach," Arn said.

"Lady downstairs wants to see you. Told her she could come up if she wanted to; we're free and easy."

"What did she say?"

"Said she had a notion to slap me."

He dressed hurriedly, climbing into the clothes that he had brought up from his scanty wardrobe at the store. He did not own a pair of low-cut shoes, and the pressure of the boot on his ankle was painful as he limped down the steep flight of stairs into the barroom. The barroom served as a lobby for the Cattleman's Rest but, since no respectable female could wait there, a closet-sized room was provided in one corner of the place. Here he found Mattie, still in what she called her working clothes—a simple dress with short sleeves, with a small white bonnet atop her pinned-up hair.

The grey eyes met his for a moment, and then flickered away.

"I'm glad you came," Arn said. "I wanted to see you."

There were only two chairs in the room; he prepared to take the other one, but Mattie came quickly to her feet.

"It's not a very comfortable place to talk," she said.

"If you're going home, I'll walk you."

"Doc needs me tonight. We've got an appendix, some granger's little boy. Doc's bringing him in now. So—"

She hesitated, shrugged, and sat down again without looking at him. Her face was an expressionless mask, and Arn felt a cold tension growing inside him. He reached out and, taking her chin in his hand, turned her face toward him.

"Mattie," he said, "you don't—"

"I think you ought to know, Arn, that I didn't exactly

89

want to come. Doc told me to. He said you'd want to see me, but that you'd be afraid to make the first move. And so he—"

"Doc can mind his own confounded business," Arn said.

"He's well-intentioned," she said sharply. "He means to help, because he always wants to help everybody. I'd do anything he asked, just because he's Doc."

There was a silence between them, filled by the bored voice of somebody calling points at a craps table in the bar.

"Mattie," Arn said abruptly, "do you think I killed Luke so I could have you?"

He had expected to shock her a little, to force some change of expression, but she must have been waiting for it. She shook her head.

"No."

"Are you sure?"

"Yes, I'm sure."

Automatically. Like somebody giving answers, rehearsed answers, to a lawyer in a courtroom. The tension had turned to agony.

"You're lying to me," he said.

"No. It's what I knew would happen, one way or the other. It doesn't make much difference how it happened."

"What you believe makes a hell of a lot of difference to me!"

"I've told you what I—"

He grabbed her hands.

"Then say it. Say it to me directly."

Her mouth trembled at the corners.

"I do not believe that you—killed—"

"Say 'I *know* you didn't—' "

"Oh, stop it, Arn!" She pulled herself away. "Stop beating on me, on yourself!"

There was no door to the room; it was closed off by a sliding curtain on a pole, and now the curtain slid open. The young woman who opened it had red hair of a peculiarly brassy sheen and a costume that was impressive from the ground to her waist and outright spectacular from her waist up. She lifted an eyebrow in apologetic surprise.

"Oh," she said. "Oh, I'm sorry. I was waiting for a fella—"

"I was going, anyhow," Mattie said.

She stopped for a moment at the door, one hand lifted to the curtain. If she had words to say, they didn't come out. She shook her head, a tight and desperate gesture, and then disappeared.

Arn got up slowly, and the redhead dropped into the chair where Mattie had sat. She crinkled her nose at the faint medicinal odor that trailed Mattie when she was fresh from the office.

"If that's the kind of perfume you like on your women, sonny," the redhead murmured, "all I got to say is, you are peculiar. But sometimes I think all men are peculiar. What do you think?"

He made no attempt to follow Mattie. Instead he limped through the bar to the stairway. A little wave of silence went ahead of him as he pushed through the crowd; talk died, and faces swung toward him, and then the talk came up again after he passed. He took the steps two at a time, despite the soreness of his ankle.

He had blown out the lamp when he left his room, but somebody had lighted it again; he saw the slice of yellow beneath the closed door. He hesitated for a moment and then, hearing the heavy breathing on the other side of the panel, let himself in.

Art Grossinger was seated on the bed, his hat on the coverlet beside him, his hands in his lap. Arn was surprised at his appearance. The man looked almost well; there was a light in his eyes where there had been a dulled shadow, and his hair was combed and his black string necktie square with the world.

"Hello, Hendricks," he said. "I want to talk to you."

"Can it wait?"

"It's important. Tonight—" Grossinger said, with a sardonic grin, "tonight I am a man."

"Meaning what?" Arn said.

"Let's get one thing straight first. I'm a good businessman. I knew more about business when I was your age than you'll know when you're eighty. If you got an impression otherwise, correct it."

Arn looked at him carefully.

"I think you're a little bit lit up," he said.

"I am. Last night brother Columbine lighted a fire without knowing it, and from time to time I've put a little oil on the wick to keep it burning. Last night I stood in that shyster's office and bowed my head and trembled, and then all of a sudden I said to myself, 'You are Arthur Grossinger, man. You have had enough of hiding in dark corners and eating dirt.' "

He cocked an eye and pointed a finger.

"I can keep better books in my head than you could keep in a roomful of ledgers, and I've kept them. Do you honestly think Ed Columbine had me bamboozled? Scared, maybe, but not bamboozled. Sit down, Hendricks."

Then, as Arn reached for the chair—

"No, wait a minute, you'd better get a pen and paper. There's a lot of this you'll want to write down."

Hendricks got them. And then, sitting on the edge of the

91

bed with his hands folded neatly in his lap, like a schoolboy reciting a familiar lesson, the cattle trader talked. He talked until after midnight.

ARN HENDRICKS WAS IN HIS STORE THE NEXT MORNING AT the regular opening time. It was the first time in two days; it seemed a week. Arn clipped the canvas gauntlets over his sleeves and went to work with the dust cloth with an energy that contained at least a small element of guilty conscience. There was plenty of dust; Railhead had caught only one edge of the storm that had struck to the south the night the posse went out. There had been a brisk shower and some lightning —one of the trail herds had lost fifty or sixty head in a minor stampede—but no real fireworks, and the searing sunlight had already burned the moisture out of the ground. Railhead's main street had turned to dust again, and the hooves of horses and the wheels of wagons kicked it up.

It was a good day for reopening. Railhead was lively this morning. Another Texas herd had arrived shortly before dark, and Joyville had spent a pyrotechnic night. And there was word around town that two more herds, totaling maybe twenty thousand head, would make it before the sun went down again. Nat Harris, who was Acting Marshal, had dug himself up a couple of emergency deputies, and with their help and a bandaged ear was trying to enforce the law.

The sodbusters were in town, too. Arn figured that it was maybe the rain; there was no other reason. But the air smelled clean and the temperature was down a little and out on the prairie there were touches of green in the bluestem gramma, and these things did something to a granger's soul. They were in and out of the store from the time Arn opened up; pricing, inspecting goods, talking with hope. But not buying. Unless he had a hidden sockful, no homesteader had anything to buy with; not this summer.

Dade was more honest than most. Arn had not even seen the man for a month; Amos Dade, who had been their neighbor when Arn and Luke were still on the claim by the river, who had lost a fine sorrel mare to McCloy. Dade scratched his whiskers and dug the toe of his clodhopper shoes into the planking of the floor and then, with an apologetic grin, spoke honestly:

"Reckon I came to get the jump on the others when it come to asking for credit. I'm going to need it, Arn. It's been a wicked summer."

"I know. None of the crops made."

"Well, the wheat did a little. About fifteen to the acre."

It was an old joke but Arn fell in with it, solemn-faced and innocent.

"Fifteen bushels an acre?"

"Nope," Dade said. "Fifteen heads."

Arn was to laugh at that line a dozen times before the day was over.

"I'll be honest with you, Amos. Your credit—and any other homesteader's—goes just as far as mine will. As long as I can get the stuff, I'll let you have it."

"Risky way to do business, isn't it?"

"Just about as risky as sod-busting, I figure. If you don't take chances on the things you believe in, you aren't much of a believer. Anyhow, I've always reckoned that if the banks and the wholesalers close me out, I can move across the tracks and sell whiskey to cowhands. Did you say something about a new doubletree?"

HE HAD TRIED TO SEE DOC CHUBB BEFORE HE OPENED UP, BUT Doc was in the country again. About eleven o'clock he saw the weather-beaten rig coming in. He made excuses to a customer and hurried out to the side of the road. Then, when he got a good look inside the buggy, he let it pass by without a hail.

Shiloh, Doc's slue-footed old black horse, was bringing him home again. Chubb was stretched out on the seat, hat over his eyes, stumpy hands folded over his paunch; he was sound asleep, and the lines were looped loosely around the empty whipsocket. This was a familiar sight in Railhead. Sometimes Doc woke up when the buggy reached its destination, sometimes not, and the citizenry also was used to the sight of Shiloh standing at the hitch rail in front of the bank, standing as if he had been nailed there, while the exhausted Doc snoozed with the racket of the street all around him.

Arn had a lot of news for Doc after last night, but he didn't have the heart to wake him up. He chirruped encouragingly at Shiloh and then turned back to the store.

He found his way blocked by a handful of men. They had formed a loose semicircle between him and the door, standing a couple of feet apart. And some of them stood with their right hands loose, swinging a little. Arn knew none of them by name, but he had seen the faces. Young faces; some of them had not felt a razor many times. This was the bunch that Railhead was beginning to call, laughingly, the Deputies, because of the way they tagged Luke Malette around.

"It's a handy thing that we found you outside, mister," one of them said. "We want to talk to you."

This one was more familiar than the rest; his face was long

93

and his skin dark with a reddish high light, as if he carried Cherokee blood. This was the one who had gun-whipped him from behind and brought a crashing end to the fight with Luke on the depot platform.

"What did you have in mind as a subject of conversation?" Arn said.

"We wanted to talk about the marshal. You remember."

"Tell him what Nat said, Jonas," said a chubby young man with a blond mustache.

"Nat Harris, who's supposed to be the law now, says he hasn't got anything to go on. That's what he said when we told him that we figured that something ought to be done about you."

Jonas' right hand had been concealed inside his loose-hanging yellow shirt; now with an easy and inconspicuous motion, he moved it into sight. The fingers of the hand tightened; there was a click, and a four-inch blade sprang from the knotted fist.

"You know why, mister. Because of what happened to the marshal."

There was no point to argument, to trying to make a denial. Arn stood silent. He was not armed; he had not worn a gun since his return from the nightmare ride that ended at Yellowhair Creek. A couple of passers-by had stopped, and there would be more of them, but they would be no help. Railhead's code in that respect was ironbound: Stay out of other people's fights, regardless of how one-sided they seem. This was based not so much on chivalry as the instinct of self-preservation.

"We thought," said Jonas, moving closer, "that maybe you would talk a little bit, to give Nat Harris something to go on."

Two more of them came around quickly and grabbed his arms, pinning them back. A man on horseback stopped to watch, leaning on his saddle horn. Jonas reached out and, taking the top button of Hendricks' coat between his thumb and the knife blade, amputated it with a single snap of his wrist.

"Now I'm through talkin'," Jonas said. "It's your turn."

He took the second button, then the third; leisurely and deliberately, as if he had all the time in the world.

"Wait a minute," said the man on horseback. "Down in Texas, this argument would look a little one-sided. Being a Texas man, I might have to step in."

"It's all right, puncher." Jonas grinned and winked at him. "This mister here is a great one for overcharging. He's the kind that doubles prices every time a new bunch of cowhands hit town. We're just fixing to lower his tariff a little bit."

94

"That," said the cowhand, "is different. If you need any help, let me know."

The knife came out again, and the black grosgrain tie that Arn wore fell away. The point of the knife dug lightly into the slack skin beneath his chin, and he felt the warm touch of blood.

Arn's stomach heaved, and his brain was alive with a strange roaring, as if there were people talking inside his head. The talking grew to an excited babble; there were shouts. Arn felt his knees wobbling, and he knew that in a moment he was going to make a fool of himself, that he was going to fall and be sick.

He sucked in his breath and flailed out blindly at the men who held him—and found that they were no longer there. The crowd was moving; somebody brushed against him and almost knocked him off his feet. Arn turned to look and, at first, saw nothing. The crowd swept him up and took him along.

A buckboard pulled by a tired work horse was coming down the middle of the street. Other traffic made way for it; horses pulled to the side, and people crossing on foot stopped in their tracks. The buckboard drew close and as it did, for an odd and unknown reason, the babble and the excitement died. In the dead silence that followed, the squeaking of the ungreased wheels of the wagon was a loud and ear-piercing sound.

There was a tarpaulin over the wagon box, covering something that pushed it up in peculiar humps. From under the tarp, near the tail gate, a pair of boots protruded stiffly. On the other side, a stockinged foot. There was a hole in the stocking. A cluster of flies followed the wagon.

The silence caved in under a roar that exploded the length of the street. There was a rush of people toward the wagon. From the tail of his eye Arn saw Mattie, her blond hair flying, her skirts held above the dust, running ahead of the rest. She was shouting a name over and over.

The man who drove the buckboard looked past her, looked into and through the crowd. His clothes were a fantastic mess; he wore no coat, and one sleeve of his shirt was ripped all the way to the cuff. But his black hair was combed and his face was shaven; he looked almost dapper.

His eyes searched the faces of Railhead until they found Arn Hendricks. And then, rising in the seat, Luke Malette lifted his arm and gave a sardonic, contemptuous salute.

Arn did not see it at all. He was looking at the yellow-haired girl, who walked now beside the buckboard with face uplifted and tears in her eyes.

RAILHEAD HAD THE STORY, AND HAD IT PRETTY STRAIGHT, BY the middle of the afternoon. After seeing to it that the bodies of the three Texans went to Chambers' Embalming Parlor to be held for inquest, Doctor Homer Chubb rescued the marshal from the crush of citizenry and hauled him off to the office for a medical going-over. Finding nothing of importance outside of fatigue, Doc sent him back to his regular quarters at the hotel, with instructions to go to bed. He did, but only after he'd been buttonholed for an hour by Mr. Ralph Coleman, editor of the Railhead *Observer*.

At the conclusion of the interview Mr. Coleman descended to the barroom of the Cattleman's Rest and, fortified with rye whiskey, proceeded to commit a journalistic oddity. He scooped himself. The regular edition of his paper was to be published in two days, but the editor couldn't wait. He told the whole thing in large and picturesque detail, and from the barroom it ran through Railhead like a fire in bacon grease.

Luke had not seen the horse again after they went under together. For a time—he had no idea how long—he had been pitched and buffeted by the water, hurled downstream with driftwood and debris. It was impossible to attempt to swim, but he was able to get his head up once or twice for a mouthful of air. He had finally got hold of a log and hung on for a distance he estimated to be a quarter of a mile. Then it threw him again, but this time the terrain was better; the banks were high, and he found a handhold among heavy roots at the water's edge. In this position he had seen Hendricks ride past him twice, on the other bank, once downstream and then up again, but he was unable to let go long enough to make a signal, and his shouting went unheard in the riot of water.

He finally found places to anchor his feet and take some of the strain off his arms, and in that position rode it out until the water began to go down, a thing that happened as suddenly as its rising. Then he pulled himself out and, on foot, took up the trail again. Shortly before dark he had commandeered a horse and dry ammunition from a homesteader's place, and before midnight he caught up with McCloy and his companions, who had made camp for the night. The marshal's theory had been right; the Texans were circling back, almost to where they came from. The showdown was less than thirty miles from Railhead. The buckboard and the plow horse belonged to a sodbuster named Ellis who came out to investigate the gunfire in the middle of the night.

Arn heard the story, or at least fragments of it, a half-dozen times before he closed the store that night. Every time it was told the same way—with innocent detachment, as if it had nothing to do with Mr. Hendricks, as if the marshal had ridden alone, and there was no question of his having a companion or of the companion's courage. The story got better, the ride on the log longer; the final version seemed to have it that the marshal emerged from the water practically at the border of the Indian Territory.

But the final footnote had to come from one man, Doctor Homer Chubb. Arn hotfooted for the office as soon as he locked his own door for the day, carrying with him a handful of closely written notes from his conversation with Grossinger the previous evening.

At the beginning, Doc didn't give him a chance to talk about it. Doc had other things on his mind; he was more upset than Arn had ever seen him before.

"I had a look," he said. "After all, I'm the coroner; it's my job. I had a look at the remains over there and—I didn't like what I saw."

"Seems to me you'd be used to that by now."

"Remains? Sure; ordinary remains, anyhow." He pulled off his spectacles and turned them nervously in his fingers. "You remember that one of McCloy's boys got a slug in him during the fight at the depot? Wasn't much of a wound, actually; upper part of the hip. But he got what we call galloping gangrene, gas gangrene. It moves like lightning; I don't see how he rode as long as he did. Anyhow, he was a plenty sick man by the time Luke caught up with him; the infection would have killed him by morning. But it didn't have a chance. He's got a bullet hole right here."

He tapped the middle of his forehead with a stubby forefinger.

"I know he was too sick to use a gun when they fought it out with Luke; I'll bet he couldn't sit up. And I suspect he wasn't even conscious."

"Then—"

Doc banged his glasses on the desk with a force that threatened to shatter them.

"I think Luke discovered that one of them was still breathing," he said bluntly, "and finished him off. Maybe it's not shocking to a lot of people; it's done. United States troopers aren't exactly famous for bringing in prisoners in the Indian fights. And there's no question this particular saddle-bum had it coming to him. Maybe six months ago I would have laughed it off."

"What do you figure to do now?"

The doctor shrugged.

"I don't know. Mention it when we get around to an inquest, and let it go at that. If it weren't for Ed Columbine, we might be able to scare Luke with this and settle him down a little. But Ed will fix things. The crowd's already made

97

Luke a hero, and Ed will bring him out of this looking like an Old Testament god of stern, swift justice."

Arn reached into his coat and brought out the sheaf of papers. He slapped them gently against his palm.

"Not exactly," he said. "Doc, do you remember when this town went crazy during the cholera epidemic? As I got it, some of the foreigners on the KP building crews ran wild and there were riots and some buildings set afire—"

"I'm not exactly the one to forget it. We finally called in a detachment from the Fort; martial law."

"I guess Art Grossinger went even crazier than the rest. He'd just lost his wife, remember. There was a mix-up over looting and a knife in some trooper's ribs and he was in real trouble."

"I don't remember that." Doc shook his head.

"You wouldn't, because Columbine fixed it. Grossinger spent twenty-four hours in a government jail and that was all. Columbine has been using it ever since; he's had the man in his pocket. Grossinger owes him a good deal of money this time, to boot."

Arn pitched the papers on the desk.

"But just awhile ago Art Grossinger said, 'Today I am a man.' We spent a long time together last night, and there's the result. And that eminent lawyer and civic leader, Ed Columbine, is going to jail."

AT SEVEN O'CLOCK THE NEXT EVENING, ARN WENT TO THE Cattleman's Rest to see Luke Malette. He did not tell Chubb what he was going to do; to Doc it would have made no sense. Arn wasn't sure that it made sense even to him, but he felt compelled to make the try.

Luke was having his dinner in the two-by-four room which passed as a dining lounge, and by a miracle there wasn't a crowd around him. Len Perro, who owned the hotel, was seated across from him. Arn moved up beside Len's chair; he did not look at Luke.

"I'm sorry, Perro, but I'd like to talk to him. It's private, but it'll only take a minute."

Perro blinked, then scrambled to his feet.

"Well, sure. I got other—"

"Stay right there, Len," Luke said, without looking up from the slab of sirloin.

"No, no, Marshal. I've got other things to do anyhow."

He scuffled away in a walk that was almost a run, and Arn grinned to himself. Perro was expecting a fight; he was probably seeing that his good whiskey was in a safe place right now.

"What bothers ˙˙ ˌuappie?"

Luke had brand-new clothes, from his boots up. His short, box-backed coat was coffee-colored; beneath it was a cream-colored waistcoat with delicate brown embroidery, and inside that a pleated white shirt.

Arn helped himself to the vacated chair.

"You're going to have to take a lot of what I'm about to say on faith, Luke. Believe me when I say I know what I'm talking about—even if I don't sound like it."

"You make even less sense than you used to."

Arn leaned across the table and spoke softly but intently:

"Luke, get away from Columbine. Give up the marshaling and break from him and let everybody know it. The best thing would be to get out of town for a while; Kansas City, maybe. You've always wanted to spend a while in Kansas City."

"What's the matter with Columbine?"

"I can't tell you. Damn it, Luke, I can't tell you anything —except that I'm talking straight and I'm thinking about your own good."

Luke put down his fork.

"If I had only a dime to my name," he said, "one silver dime, between me and starvation, I'd be willing to stake it that you're not doing anything for my good."

"Have it your way. Make it simple. Forget what I said about Columbine. Just get out for a while. You've got to."

Luke leaned back in his chair, and the movement of his hand was almost casual; there was nothing hurried about it as he lifted the gun and laid it on the table.

"I'm not heeled," Arn said levelly. "I want to talk, not to fight."

"You sounded like you were trying to order me out of town. I just wanted to make sure that you didn't get serious." The cold, one-sided smile crawled up his cheek. "There's one thing I guess you don't understand, chappie. This is my town. It belongs to me. Maybe somebody else has got the deeds and the titles; maybe they put their names on their hardware stores. But I run it, and it's my town. And nobody orders me out."

"Listen, Luke—"

"You've got it all backwards. I give the orders. Like this." The nose of the gun lifted, looking over the top of the salt and pepper shakers. "Get away from me. You're ruining my dinner."

Arn laughed and pushed back his chair.

"Can't you do anything without the help of your penny pistol, Marshal? Sometimes I think it must grow at the end of your arm," he said. "It settles all arguments, solves all problems. It thinks for you."

As he got up, his eye was caught by a flicker of subdued color. Glittering against the white lawn of Luke's sleeve was a small round opal.

"Uh-huh," drawled the marshal, following Arn's glance. "I got my cuff links back."

THE FADED PHOTOGRAPH HAD THE PLACE OF HONOR ON THE mahogany bureau. It sat atop the crocheted runner, smack in the middle, flanked by a pair of hairbrushes on one side and a sea shell containing fancy shirt studs on the other.

The visitor applied flame to the end of his cheroot and inspected the cold-eyed boy who held the Springfield with certain amusement. To Mr. Columbine, there was something peculiar about a man who kept a picture of himself in his boudoir. Just as there was something amusing in the full-length mirror which Luke had requested, and which now graced the wall opposite the windows.

There were boot heels in the hall outside and the door came open.

"Maybe I don't like people hanging around my room," Luke said.

"Oh, tut-tut, boy." Mr. Columbine grinned. "I came to say hello, and when I found the door unlatched I figured you'd be back shortly. So I waited. Good dinner?"

"It was until Arn butted in."

"What did Hendricks have to say?"

"It sounded like nothing, but it might have been a lot." Luke took the brushes from the bureau and faced the mirror. "Ed, are you crooked?"

Columbine laughed.

"That's a delicate question to ask an attorney. We're a sensitive profession." Then the dry laughter went out of his voice. "Did Hendricks say I was?"

"Damned if I know what he said," Luke grunted, brushing. "But he gave me some ideas, very funny ideas. He seems to think you're in trouble. And I got the idea that he thinks that means I'm in trouble, too. Like I was the tail and you the puppy dog."

"Ha!" Columbine said. "Very funny."

The cold eyes searched his face.

"I'd hate to think I'd been working with a crook," Luke said softly. "Get it straight—I'm nobody's boy. I never was and I never will be. But you got me hired and you've loaned me money and, well, been on my side. I'd hate to think I'd been helping you pull something without even knowing it."

"Who's pulling anything?" Columbine said, a little irritably. "Are you simpleton enough to believe anything Hendricks tells you?"

Luke gave his hair a final inspection and then sauntered over to the bureau and got a polishing cloth from the bottom drawer.

"I've got nothing in particular against crookedness," he said. "This is country where a man has to use his head or eat dust. I wouldn't even mind if people thought we were crooks together."

He cocked his boot on the edge of the attorney's chair and, with a casual gesture, tossed the cloth in his lap.

"But I won't be used," he said. "And I won't have people thinking that I'm used. Particularly not by a fat-bottomed lawyer with ink under his fingernails. Give the heel a couple of swipes, will you?"

Columbine stiffened and his fingers dug into the arm of the chair, but only for a moment. Then, with a thin smile, he dabbed at the heel of the boot.

"You worry a lot about what people think, don't you?" he said. "That's the way it should be; you're a big man, a man in the public eye. So it seems to me that, instead of making bad guesses about the morals of your friends, you ought to be working on some mouths that flap too much in this town."

The boot dropped to the floor with a bang.

"Meaning what?"

"Meaning that various people say various things. Such as, Arn Hendricks was beating the daylights out of you that day at the depot until some of your friends saved your skin. Such as, any man's a big man when he's holding a gun. Such as—"

"Who says it?" The words were quiet, the eyes cold circles.

"That's only a few people, understand. Most of the citizens in this town are all for you, boy. They think—"

"Name the people!"

"Well—a man like Art Grossinger isn't really responsible, of course. He's sick, his nerves are gone. He stands with his foot on the bar over at the Paris Girl and talks just to have something to do. The way some people whittle." The lawyer shrugged; his eyebrows went up. "But," he added judicially, "he does talk."

"Would he be there tonight?"

"The Paris Girl? Probably."

Luke took his new brown hat from the bed and carefully put it on, inspecting himself in the mirror.

"Now, wait a minute," Columbine said. "It's not that urgent. It can wait until you run into Art again; you can drop a little hint—"

"I think I'll do it tonight," Luke said.

Once again Columbine shrugged.

"Suit yourself. Only—don't kick up a ruckus, Marshal. Just talk to him. You know."

"I know," Luke said, and closed the door.

Mr. Columbine leaned back in the chair and yawned, stretching his arms over his head. He examined the tip of his cigar. It had gone out, and he scowled. After a search of his vest, he finally found a match in his coat pocket. He relighted, taking a good deal of time about it, tasting the smoke with relish. Then he got up and walked over to the bureau.

He flipped the burnt match from his finger tips, and it struck the picture with a soft slap and then bounced off to the floor. Mr. Columbine put his hat on and leisurely made his way out and downstairs.

THE BARROOM WHICH SERVED AS A LOBBY FOR THE CATTLE-man's Rest was jammed, and the crap and faro tables were invisible in the tangle of customers. Two hundred more cowhands, fresh from the trail, had come into Railhead during the day. One of them was now attempting to walk the length of the bar with a shot glass of whiskey balanced on his chin. Two more were attempting to help Nervous Freddie, the frayed-looking fiddle player, to render "Annie Lisle."

Mr. Columbine patiently worked his way into the mob at the craps table, won eighty dollars in side bets on a bony Texan who shot three consecutive sevens, and worked his way out again. He stood on the board sidewalk outside for a time, lighting a new cheroot and enjoying a comfortable sense of well-being. He joined in the general laughter at a cowhand who attempted to ride a pony into the post office and found the door too narrow. And then, finally, he wandered back to his office. His office was as good a place as any to wait.

There was a light under Doc Chubb's door, but he gave it no more than passing notice. The good doctor would be busy for quite a stretch now; if he got more than four hours' sleep in the next twenty-four, he could consider himself lucky.

Mr. Columbine was just turning his key in the lock when Doc's door came open. The lawyer turned, prepared to offer an amiable hello, but something in the faces of the two men who came out suggested that it was not the time for pleasantries. Nat Harris, who was once again an ordinary deputy since the marshal's return, looked stern and apologetic and frightened, all at the same time.

But there was nothing apologetic or frightened about Homer Chubb. Doc just looked businesslike.

"Go ahead, Nat. Now's as good a time as any."

Nat, a moonfaced young man with the beginnings of a red beard, hitched at his gun belt and took a step forward. He made a couple of false starts before he finally got it out.

"Mister," he said, "you're under arrest."

The creak of the deputy's boots as he shifted his feet was the only sound for a long moment. Columbine did not even look at Harris.

"Is it a joke, Homer?"

"If you'll give me those handcuffs, Nat, I'll show him how funny it really is. Just put out your hands, Ed."

"Arrest for what?" the lawyer said hoarsely.

"Fraud, maybe. Embezzlement—misuse of public funds. You'd know the language better than I would. Anyhow, we got it figured at about twenty thousand dollars in the last thirty-two months."

"Is there a warrant?"

"There is." Doc nodded his head patiently. "I swore it out and Nat, here, fixed it up." He crooked a finger. "The hands, Ed."

Mr. Columbine slowly extended them.

"This town may grow up yet," Doc said. "You realize, lawyer, that this is the first time I can remember any charge like this in court around here? It's always been murder or drunkenness or disturbing the peace. All very low-brow offenses. I guess we ought to be grateful to you for giving the place a little class."

"I think I know where you got your information," Columbine said, "and it's not worth a damn. You'll never get a case."

"I figure the government will help with that. There's federal money mixed up in it, too, if you'll think back. Hay cut from public lands and sold to the cavalry, out at the Fort, for one thing. We wired Kansas City, and we figure on having a U. S. marshal here tomorrow. Meanwhile, we got a bed for you overnight. Public bed with a public mattress, Ed."

The door at the bottom of the stairway banged open.

"Hey, Doc!"

The boy in the door, down at the street level, was out of breath. He had delivered this kind of news before, for he was the son of the proprietor of the Paris Girl Saloon. But, because he was only thirteen, he still got excited about it.

"We got one, Doc," he called up to Chubb.

Doc nodded wearily.

"I'll get my bag and be right with you."

"You don't need to come to our place, Doc. He's mackereled. Some of the boys are taking him to Chambers' already. But Pop thought you ought to know."

"All right. Got any idea who it is?"

"Don't know his name, but he's around town. He breathes funny." The boy slapped himself on the chest and panted. "You know."

Doc Chubb turned and looked at Columbine.

"The marshal did it," said the voice from the stairs. "Boy, the marshal's been a busy man, last few days. If you know what I mean."

"All right," Doc said. "All right." His eyes met the lawyer's briefly and then moved to the deputy. "You put him away, Nat. And then get over there and see what you can find out. I'll get my gear and see you at the undertaker's."

HOMER CHUBB, AGE TWENTY-ONE, HAD GONE SICK AT HIS stomach the first time he saw a corpse on the dissecting table at the Eclectic Institute of Medical Learning. So did most of his classmates. Like them, Homer Chubb soon grew out of it and developed a clinical detachment. The War and the field at Cold Harbor removed even that, and substituted the tired boredom of a trash collector who has more material than he can handle. It was good training for the frontier and for Kansas. During the cholera epidemic, shortly after Railhead's founding, there had come a nightmare time when the only thing left to do was burn, like the heathen on the Ganges, and Doc had had to do it alone.

And now he had come the circle. Now, maybe he was getting old. Because as he pulled up the sheet and began to roll down his sleeves in the flickering butter-colored light of the coal-oil lamp, Doc Chubb realized that he was sick at his stomach in the presence of the dead again.

He did not actually hear Nat Harris, the deputy, come into the room; when he looked up, Nat was there.

"I went over and asked around some," he said. He teetered uncomfortably, and his boots squeaked. "A lot of people saw it happen, and, of course, everybody tells it his own way. Anyhow there was an argument—Luke seemed to think that this fella here had been running him down, talking behind his back—and the first thing anybody knew, they were both pulling. Lot of argument about who pulled first. Anyhow—"

"Anyhow, I can tell you the rest of it," Doc Chubb said. "Grossinger wore a little armpit gun. He got it out, but before he could fire, Luke put a slug through his hand. Did you find the Grossinger gun?"

The deputy patted his pocket.

"Luke's first shot disarmed his man; very skillful shooting. The second shot, immediately afterward, was through the left chamber of the heart. Also skillful." Doc spoke mechanically, almost as if the recitation bored him. "The first shot was possibly self-defense. The second shot was murder. Murder as outright as if he'd come behind him in the dark and shot him through the back."

Harris scuffled his feet against the raw planking of the floor.

"Well—"

"That's what the witnesses said, isn't it?—first the hand, then the heart?"

Harris nodded.

So far as Doc was concerned, that ended the conversation. He turned abruptly and walked over to the small table in the corner that held a washbasin. His detachable cuffs were looped over the towel rack; he took them down and, taking the links from the table, put the cuffs back on. It took him longer than usual to do this, because his hands were unsteady. Then he reached for his coat.

"All right," he said. "All right. I guess we need another warrant."

It took a minute for it to sink in.

"You mean—for the marshal?" Harris stammered.

"He committed the murder, didn't he? And the fact that he is the marshal has nothing to do with it. It was a private fight."

"But you can't just up and swear out a warrant—"

"I'm the coroner of this county, and on the basis of medical evidence I want Luke Malette arrested."

Harris wiped his mouth with the back of his hand.

"I couldn't do that, Doc. I—I'm a friend of Luke's. I work with him."

Doc looked him up and down.

"Besides which you're scared to death of him," he said quietly, and smiled. There was no contempt in the smile; it was understanding, almost affectionate. "All right, Nat. You go back to the jail and keep an eye on lawyer Columbine."

Doc snapped his bag shut and got his hat from the peg on the wall. Harris watched him, frowning a little; he did not move until Chubb brushed against him on the way to the door.

"Where you going now, Doc?"

"I've got business of my own to attend to."

A cool breeze had swung into the town, and Doc stopped for a moment on the sidewalk just to taste the good air. Then he padded briskly across the street, dodging the traffic that was just hitting its peak, and down to the bank building. He was puffing by the time he reached the top of the stairs; he stopped for a moment to catch his breath, and then let himself in through the door that led directly to his working quarters. The lamp above his desk was still burning; he had forgotten to blow it out.

He seated himself at the desk and ran a stubby thumb and forefinger into the bottom pocket of his vest. The small brass key glinted in the lamplight. He bent over the lowest drawer and grunted with satisfaction as he threaded the key into the lock. His han. ⁴ was steady now.

There was a smell of grease and leather in the drawer, a good smell. He unwrapped the belts carefully from around the matched Peacemakers; the lamplight turned the silver and ivory to gold. Doc ran his finger along the intricate design of the butt plate, like a blind man who reads by his sense of touch.

Then he got up and hooked the belts around his hips and moved the guns in their holsters. They slid easily; the limp black cloth was as soft as a woman's hand. He checked the load by turning each .44 to the light, so that the brass rims of the cartridges were visible in the breech. Both cylinders were full.

He leaned across the desk and cupped his hand above the chimney of the lamp and blew it out and then hurried down the stairs to the street.

"I'm looking for the marshal," he said to a couple of cowhands who stood on the sidewalk. "You gentlemen see anything of him?"

IT WAS NOT UNUSUAL FOR THE WESTBOUND TRAIN OF THE Kansas Pacific to be even a full day late. But the fact that it was two hours late on this particular night did have, perhaps, a certain ironic aspect. Because it was at the depot that Doctor Homer Chubb finally caught up with Luke Malette and tried to arrest him.

The doctor approached the platform from the darkness at the south end of the station. In contrast to the general shadowiness of the town the platform seemed almost glaring, and he had a chance to watch Luke as he approached.

One surprising thing he saw immediately. Luke was alone, and he was never seen alone in a public place any more; he was tagged after like an actress. But tonight the usual collection of idle citizenry had left a small island of vacancy around him. He leaned against the wall, his feet crossed, his pocketed hands holding his coat open. Even the hooligans that Railhead called the Deputies were not around.

It was not a matter of neglect through oversight. The people on the platform knew the marshal was there; sometimes a look went in his direction and then flicked away again, and much of the talk was low-throated and quiet. There had been a mob at the Paris Girl Saloon; the Grossinger story was all over town by now.

Sooner or later, Doc thought, *every man of violence gets a mark on him, and the mark is like a wall, keeping his fellow men away. Can it happen as quick as that? Can it happen in an hour?*

It seemed to Doc—his imagination, probably—that even Luke knew it; that there was a coiled tension in the motionless figure against the wall.

Doc stopped at the edge of the light and lifted the gun from his right holster. It was insane to try to draw with the marshal. He let the gun hang at arm's length, pressed against his leg as he walked stiffly across the platform.

Somebody else moved out of the shadow and overtook him, moving up on the other side.

"Doc, what's the matter with you? What are you doing down here?"

Arn Hendricks was on the wrong side to see the gun.

"Might ask you that," Doc said.

"I'm supposed to have a shipment of goods on this thing tonight, if it ever gets here. You know. Business."

"Me too," Doc said. "I'm here on business."

His walk became a fast shuffle, leaving Arn behind. Luke had seen him now; his face was lost in the shadow of the hat rim, but he cocked his head and straightened a little. Doc waited until he was close, not more than ten feet, and then lifted the gun.

"Marshal," he said, "I'm going to have to ask you to put up your hands. You're under arrest."

As he said it, an absurd but terrifying notion entered his mind. What if Luke thought it was funny and simply laughed at him? They might all laugh; Doc was aware that there had been a good deal of sniggering over his hardware before. If they laughed, what did he do?

Luke Malette didn't think it was funny.

"You're mistaken, Doctor," he said softly. "You can't arrest me."

"Don't josh yourself. As the coroner, I'm an officer of the law. You're under arrest for the murder of Arthur Grossinger, on the orders, I suspect, of Ed Columbine. It's within my authority."

"I don't care about your authority. You're mistaken."

"In a pig's eye," said a voice from the group that stood frozen around them. "I saw that shooting, Doc; it was cold."

107

"He's right," Luke said. The words were a monotone. "It was cold. But you aren't going to arrest me. My name is Malette, and there's nobody in the state of Kansas big enough to arrest me. Least of all a twittery old man who carries guns without knowing what they're for."

"Try me and see," Doc said.

This time Luke laughed; his face, at least, although no sound came out.

"You carried those things around this town for years and never fired them once," he said. "Not once. Did you, Doctor?"

Chubb felt his tongue go thick. He could not answer. And the hand that held the .44 had a violent tremble. He tightened his grip.

"I don't think you could hold a gun on a man and pull the trigger," Luke went on. "Why, I'll bet you'd stand right there and let me reach—"

His hand dropped leisurely to his hip.

"—and draw—"

There was a flash of metal in the light.

"—and cock—"

Doc's brain screamed a frantic message to an arm that was completely dead.

"—and without even touching the trigger, you water-livered old fool, you'd let me pull—like *this!*"

The marshal was mistaken. Chubb did get a shot off; the slug tore into the platform at his feet. Perhaps he did not fire consciously. The impact of lead in his body may have finally tripped a secret trigger his mind had been unable to reach. He took two slugs in the chest, no farther apart than the spread of a man's hand, and fell face down.

Luke Malette stepped up and looked at him for a moment. Then he lifted his head and smiled crookedly at the crowd.

"Do you honestly suppose he thought he could arrest me?" he said, like a puzzled child. And then, without waiting for an answer, he turned and disappeared into the depot.

Nobody noticed—if, indeed, there was even anybody to remember—that Doctor Homer Chubb fell and bled out his life on almost exactly the same spot where he had first set foot on the soil of the brand-new town called Railhead.

NOBODY WHO SAW IT HAPPEN BELIEVED IT FOR A WHILE. People who got it secondhand, after the word began to spread, accepted it without question. But men who had the testimony of their own eyes stood and stared foolishly, first at the dumpy figure crumpled on the platform and then at one another, without speaking. There was a long frozen moment after Luke Malette passed out of sight before anybody even made a move toward Doc. Arn Hendricks was the first, and then a couple of others.

Even then, most of them continued to stand and stare. "Did you see—?" they whispered to one another. "He just—"

"Now, wait a minute—"

"Papa, I can't see. Lift me, Papa—"

Arn Hendricks and the others rolled Doc over and then carefully picked him up and started toward the depot with him. And finally the crowd came to.

"Where's Malette?" came an angry shout.

That tore it wide open. The crowd disintegrated in a burst of movement. Guns bounced from holsters; men swarmed over the depot and piled in—and then out—of it through every door that was open. When they found one on the east side that was locked, half a dozen shoulders drove against it in a frenzy and knocked it in. There was nothing inside except oil and grease and wiping rags; they pitched them angrily on the platform. Inside, a chorus of voices shouted angry questions at the dispatcher.

He couldn't tell them much. The marshal had walked through the building, gone out the far door, and disappeared into the street. They went roaring through the same door, into the same street.

It was the beginning of a fantastic night in Railhead. That night nobody slept. Angry men ranged through the town. They carried lanterns and ropes and ax handles and every variety of firearm from fourteen-pound buffalo guns to six-ounce derringers. Not a half-dozen houses in town escaped invasion. Around midnight there was a story that Luke had been seen going into the darkened church, and a mob took the key from a terrified Reverend Minner and searched the chapel, beating among the pews like men searching game in underbrush.

Everybody had a theory. At least three impromptu posses rode out, not so much on specific leads as on the general notion that a man on the run will go for the open country. To other people this made no sense at all. Arn Hendricks supplied some of the posse members with ammunition, but he did not ride with them. Arn was certain in his bones that Luke was still in town.

It made more sense that way. Railhead was not a big town, either in terms of buildings or space. But, beyond its normal population, it was jammed tonight with close to five hundred strangers. In a dark tangle of humanity where a man can see only if he carries his light with him there is a lot of room to move without detection. And so Arn, like a hundred others, walked the streets with a gun in one hand and a lantern in the other.

It was doubtful if Doc Chubb would have seen it that way, but this was probably the greatest mass tribute Railhead could ever give a man. Those who do the healing are deep in the foundations of any community; Doc had been the only physician Railhead had ever had, and a frontier community is very close to its doctor. He had touched, in one way or another, the lives of every citizen of the town and the plow-scarred area around it. He had given three times as much service as he had ever been paid for. And so Railhead paid him now, in a grim-eyed frenzy that was more like a riot than a search.

AT APPROXIMATELY ONE FIFTEEN IN THE MORNING LUKE Malette made a brief appearance at a public building in the heart of town. He was seen, however, by only one man, who was unable to tell about it later. The public building was the jail. The man was Edward Columbine.

Despite the racket in the streets, Mr. Columbine, who was a man with an abundance of self-control, had been dozing for the past hour. He was awakened by the banging of the door that led into the miniature cell block. He sat up, scowling in annoyance. It was probably Nat Harris, who had been in and out a dozen times during the night. There was no regular jailer on duty.

The light was poor and his eyes muddy with sleep, so he had to blink a few times before he recognized the marshal. The look of annoyance increased.

"You better stay on the move. Don't you know this whole town's out for your scalp?"

"I know it. But I wanted to see you, lawyer."

Columbine grunted.

"If you came down here to release me, no thanks," he said. "The thought is appreciated, but I'm staying right where I am. I can talk myself out of this foolish business in a court of law, and I don't intend to get mixed up in any roughhouse foolishness like a jail break. Your mental processes have always been a little on the gaudy side, Marshal."

"I didn't come to let you out," Luke said. For the first time Columbine noticed that he had a gun in his hand. "I thought I knew why I shot Grossinger tonight at the time it happened. But I didn't. I found out later. Didn't I tell you nobody used me, lawyer?"

His tone was patient, as if he spoke to an erring child. He moved a step closer to the bars that separated them.

"You were crooked, too. I told you that you'd better not be crooked, didn't I?"

There was only one other cell in the small stone building. It was full, but the three cowhands who occupied it were out cold in a rotgut stupor. It would do no good to yell. The town was full of yelling.

The gun came up; its round snout came through the bars.

"I just came to settle up, lawyer."

Mr. Columbine yelled anyhow. Or tried to. The flash and thunder came before the scream left his lungs.

ARN HENDRICKS HAD RETURNED TO HIS STORE ABOUT MID-night—as soon as his normal thinking processes began to function again. For a while he had done the same as every-body else; walked the street blindly with a gun in his hand, his mind a red blaze of anger, looking twice at every shad-ow. He had walked alone. so far as it was possible to be alone in that tangle, fightir ɜ a foolish impulse to shout at the rest of them to go home, that this was his fight; that it was private, and they intruders upon his responsibilities. Perhaps it was the walking that cooled him. The red blaze died and the cold pattern of logic replaced it.

He had returned to the store and lighted the lamp on the upended packing box that served as his desk; his books were there, and the cashbox. The light could be seen from the street. He had arranged the stool so that he could keep an eye on both the front and back door, and for a long time he had sat quietly, waiting.

Then his eye caught the small shipping carton behind the counter. It had arrived on the morning train. From the label he knew what it contained, and he had not opened it. At the time he had been almost afraid to. But now he got up and carried it over to the light and pulled it apart with a claw hammer.

The Peacemakers, wrapped in an oiled cloth, were packed in wood shavings. Some of the shavings spilled to the floor, and he picked them up carefully before he unwrapped the guns.

The yellow of the coal-oil light gave the silver a golden cast, and the barrels and breeches glinted from a thin coat of grease. He fetched a cloth and cleaned them up, sighting through each of the chambers in the cylinders to make cer-tain they were clear. Then he loaded them and placed them side by side on the desk. The blank ivory handles, uncarved, looked curiously nude.

The knock that came on the front door was light and hurried; his hand moved toward the desk, and then stopped.

111

Luke was not likely to knock and, if he did, it wouldn't be like that.

"It's me, Arn."

He hurried down the aisle between the counters and let her in. She was dressed plainly, the way she dressed for Doc's office, but there was no small white bonnet, and her hair was down.

"You should be in bed," he told her stiffly.

"Is anybody expected to sleep on a night like this?"

"The sleeping is up to you, but you shouldn't be on the street alone. It's wild tonight."

"Yes," she whispered. "It's wild. Arn, did they find him?"

"Not yet, but they will. Somebody will. Now go back to the Reverend's. You can't stay here."

"Do you figure you'll find him, Arn?"

"Maybe. If I do, I'll do exactly what anybody else would. Make up your mind to it, Mattie."

"I've already done that." The grey eyes, gazing levelly into his, looked black in the light. "What do you think Luke means to me?"

"Does it make a difference?"

"I want to know what you think."

His eyes moved away from hers and hung in the far shadows of the room.

"I saw you when he came in with the buckboard. I saw you on the run, calling." Suddenly he reached for her arm and pushed her toward the door. "Get out of here."

"Why? Because it's not proper for a young lady to be alone with a gentleman in a hardware store in the middle of the night?"

"Just go, Mattie!"

"Or is it because you expect Luke to come here?" she said quietly. "Because you realized that it was foolish to try to find him—when he would come to find you?"

They were standing almost in the center of the store, facing the street, with the desk behind them. Arn heard the movement at the back door and started to turn, but the voice came immediately:

"Stay there. Right there, chappie. Did you know the back door was unlocked?"

"I was hoping you'd come in," Arn said. "It wouldn't have made much sense to bolt it, considering."

"That's a good answer," Luke said. "Mattie, reach over and unbuckle his gun belt."

She hesitated; her eyes searched Arn's.

"Do what he says."

She fumbled for a moment and the .38 thudded to the floor.

"Now you can turn around."

He had got hold of a slicker somewhere, to cover the gaudy clothes; the band of lamplight touched the shapeless black stuff as high as the waist, but above that everything was in shadow.

"I was wondering—is this the pair I ordered, here on the desk?"

"They came this morning."

Luke took a fast step forward and scooped them up, then moved back again.

"I'm a little short on the ready cash, Arn, but I'll settle up with you. You can count on it. Now I want you to do a couple of things. Move slow, and don't be foolish and try to argue. Get two dishpans, big ones."

"Dish—"

"I said not to argue!" The words cracked like a whip.

Arn slid behind the counter and took them from the shelf.

"One under each arm," Luke said. "So that I know your hands are full. That's good. Now come on. We've got to ride."

"Luke!" Mattie said. "Luke, don't take him with you. Let him stay here; we won't say anything, neither of us will say—"

"She's talking only for herself," Arn said sharply. "I'm not making any bargains."

He moved around the desk, his arms spread awkwardly over the bulky pans, and the gun barrel waved him on to the door. He caught the moist sound of horses' breathing. The marshal pushed open the door.

"Luke!" she said, and there was a frantic tightness in her voice. "I don't know where you're going or what you're doing to him—but don't—Luke, for my sake. I meant something to you once."

"Did you, Mattie?" he said. "Maybe you did. There was a time when there was a hole in my world, when I needed people to plug up the gap, before we came West. I suppose you were a big help, Mattie, and I thank you for it. But I don't need anybody now. And nobody means anything to me. Nobody; get it straight."

He reached out with one hand, opened the gate on the lantern that stood on the table, and quickly blew it out. The room sank into blankness.

"Arn," Mattie said. Her voice was level. "The day you saw me running out to meet the buckboard, there was one thing that kept going over and over in my head—*Arn didn't kill him after all. Arn is not a killer. Thank God.* I was glad to see him—but for your sake, not his."

113

"We're in a hurry," Luke said. He took the lantern in his free hand. "We'll need this, chappie. Now hurry."

The muzzle of the gun drove sharply into Arn's spine.

"Arn—"

"I'll be back, Mattie. Now you go home and go to bed. I'll be back."

He heard Luke's chuckle behind him as they stepped outside. It was a dry laugh, but not humorless. The marshal honestly seemed a little amused.

THERE WAS A STRONG TOUCH OF IRONY THROUGHOUT THE happenings of that night, and one of the most ironic was the fact that when Luke Malette and Arn Hendricks rode out of town they went squarely down the middle of the street, with the horses at a casual trot. Arn rode ahead, with Luke beside and slightly behind him. There had been no cautioning words, no threats; Hendricks knew without prompting that his only hope of staying alive was to behave himself. They were passed by dozens of people, some of them so close that Arn, if his hands had been free, could have reached out and touched them. They were not even challenged. Perhaps the fact that there were two of them had something to do with it; everybody expected Malette to be alone. And the ludicrousness of a man riding with an armful of dishpans disarmed any remaining suspicion.

The traffic thinned as they approached the edge of the town, and Luke pulled up until they rode side by side.

"They're all looking for me," he said. There was hurt wonder in his voice. "Every damn one of them." He snorted. "By Judas, I don't believe it. I'll bet if I went back there and walked down the street and told them who I was, they'd—they'd—"

"Kneel and give thanks?" Arn said sardonically. "Try it and see."

"This town belongs to me, don't they know that?" His voice rose above the subdued racket. "Wait a minute; we pull in here."

The ungainly two-story bulk of the Exchange, the frame building which was the nerve center of the cattle trade, loomed ahead of them. It was completely dark; the nearest light was down at the sales platform, where the night crew had their quarters.

"Get a match and strike it," Luke said. "Move careful."

Arn awkwardly shifted the pans and obeyed. The tiny flame stood upright and unwavering; no breeze moved tonight. The air was close and sultry. Luke extended the lantern.

"Light it. And remember there's still a gun in the other hand."

Arn thrust the match through the open chimney gate. The wick had been turned high; it snapped into a hot flame. Luke kicked his horse close to the building and rose in his stirrups. He swung his arm; the lantern arced over his head and hurtled through an open window into the guts of the building.

"Luke, what do you think you're—"

"This is a start, anyhow. The bank would have been nice, but I'm afraid the bank wouldn't burn. Now let's see how fast these nags can go. Straight on, chappie!"

He smacked the rump of Arn's horse with the flat of his hand. The pony almost jerked the saddle from under him as it bolted ahead. They pounded down the trail at a dead gallop.

The ground rose here; not enough to be considered a hill, but nevertheless a definite rise. Railhead was built at the end of a broad and shallow draw. The roadbed of the Kansas Pacific, and the trail beside it, ran along the bottom. At the highest point, a mile from the edge of town, the shoulders on either side were thirty feet above the bottom, and the whole formation perhaps as much as three hundred feet above the level of the distant town. From here, it was downhill all the way to Railhead.

This area was thick with longhorns. The whole county was one vast bedding ground of Texas beef, waiting to be moved to the loading pens and eastbound freight cars. As the riders crested the rise, the dull gloss of thousands of horns in the crystal blueness of the night turned the prairie to a sea. Luke pulled alongside Arn and signaled a stop.

"Now what?"

"I think we'll cut in here, over to the right. Just follow your nose, chappie. At a slow walk."

There was a stretch of open grass between two clusters of cattle here, like a road cut through a forest. They moved cautiously along it. Arn had stopped trying to guess what was in Luke's mind. None of this made sense to him yet, but he knew it would; it would make diabolical sense.

The cattle nearest them, a couple of rods away on either side, stirred uncomfortably. The pathway narrowed and curved and twisted; sometimes it almost closed. The ground was still rising as they approached the top of the shoulder.

"How many head in this bunch?" Luke whispered, with a wave to the right, toward town.

"I don't know anything about cattle. Five hundred head, maybe."

They were on the top now, the draw below and behind

them. The natural movement of the cattle had left this ridge bare. They pulled their horses around so that they looked down on the animals through which they'd just made their way. There was a general movement in the mass now. The longhorns were getting spooky.

"Five hundred head," Luke murmured. "I guess it's enough. At least for a start." He laughed softly, deep in his throat. "Now do you know why I brought you out here, chappie? I wasn't sure I could get them started—alone."

The truth hit Arn like a hammer blow, almost physically; he rocked backward in the saddle. Stampeding cattle run blindly, with no sense of direction; they run exactly like water, following the easiest way, where the shape of the land leads them. A sudden commotion on this ridge would send every animal between them and the railroad plunging down the slope—and the shoulders of the draw would funnel them in a roaring flood toward town. Toward town, through its streets, and even beyond.

"You've heard boys say that when they go, they intend to take somebody with them? I'm bigger than that. I'm taking a town with me."

Arn tried to speak, but he could not; he could not even breathe.

"All right," Luke said, and rose suddenly in his stirrups. "Bang your dishpans, chappie! Dishpans ought to make a fine lot of racket!"

He lifted his hands high over his head. There was a gun in each hand, and two shots split the night.

"Yee-hooooooooooo!" he shrieked. "Yi-yi-yi-yi-hooooooo!"

Thirty feet away an old bull, already moving, reared like a bronco and bawled in terror.

"I said to bang them!" Luke shouted. "Damn you, move!"

His right-hand gun did not fire in the air this time. Arn found himself looking directly into the flash and something hissed hotly past his cheek. Later he was to be grateful for that; it knocked him awake, out of the frozen horror that held him. Without thinking, he made the only resistance he could make. With a clumsy motion he pitched one of the pans toward the other rider.

It fell short and landed directly in front of the horse which Malette rode, hitting the ground with a tinny clatter and then rolling. It rolled against the stallion's flanks.

A dozen gunshots would not have produced half the effect. The horse did not rear; he jumped like a scared cat, all four feet off the ground, his back arched, shrieking with fright. Luke was still half-standing in the stirrups. He dropped the guns and made a frantic attempt to grab leather, but by that

116

time he was sailing over the stallion's ears. He landed rolling, ten feet away.

Arn lunged out of his saddle, took two steps, and then landed on top of him. The earth beneath them quivered violently, and the world was full of thunder. The longhorns were running.

If the fall dazed the marshal at all, it was only for a moment. He clawed at Hendricks' face, going for the eyes. Arn fought the hand away and swung his own fist at the shadowy shape of Luke's head. His knuckles dug into the hard earth, and an instant later a knee came upward, into his groin. He lurched forward, engulfed by a convulsive wave of pain.

For a moment they tore at each other silently, belly to belly, their bodies twisted together. Then, very lightly, something touched Arn's ribs and slid under his skin. There was no particular pain, but a frightening coldness shot through him. Suddenly, lifting his arm took more strength than he could muster. His head rocked.

He had forgotten about the knife that always rode in the top of Luke's boot.

He tried to stand up; he got as far as his knees, and that was all. Luke scrambled away. Arn felt the movement, rather than saw it, as he pitched forward again.

It seemed that he stood at the edge of a yellow pool, as yellow as the sun, and there was a warm and pleasant something that tried to pull him in. He fought against it.

Get up, he told himself. *Get up. He'll finish you anyhow.*

He knew that the yellow pool was part of his pain, his imagination. But the painful lump pressing against his stomach was real. He was lying on something. He lifted himself on one elbow enough to slide his hand in, and his fingers curled around a gun butt.

"Yi-yi-yi-yi-yi-yi!"

The yell and the tinny clatter were just audible above the uproar that shook the earth. Arn rolled over. Standing on the ridge, his feet spread and his head thrown back, was Luke Malette. He had a gun in one hand and a dishpan in the other, and he was banging them together and shouting at the sky like a playful, triumphant child.

Arn sat up and lifted the gun to eye level. His finger moved to the trigger and then stopped.

No. Not that way.

He pulled in all the breath he could manage.

"Luke!" he shouted hoarsely.

Malette heard it. He came around fast, pulling the Peacemaker down and firing in the same motion. The slug kicked dirt beside the hip of the man who sat hunched in the bluestem with his gun hand propped against his knee and the sight of the other Colt at eye-level. Before the marshal could fire again, Arn Hendricks pulled the trigger.

Malette fell face down, and the dishpan bounced against the ground and rolled away. Arn crawled on his hands and knees to where Luke lay. There was no need to roll the body over. Arn had known where the slug would hit before he pulled the trigger.

"Luke." His mouth formed the word soundlessly. "Luke."

LATER, USING THE KNIFE THAT LAY IN THE GRASS, HE CUT through the bound edge of his coat, so that the fabric would tear, and then ripped off a handful of patches. These he stuffed inside his shirt, over the knife wound, until the wad was big enough so the tightness of the shirt fabric would hold them in place. His head was clearing.

He had no idea where Luke had got the horse which he had brought for him to ride; probably off a hitch rail somewhere. The choice had been a good one. It was some Texan's cow pony, trained to discipline and accustomed to uproar. Luke's stallion was nowhere in sight, but the little horse still stood where the reins had dropped.

Arn got up and looked around him. It was like standing on an island in the midst of a running tide. The longhorns, bolting from the thing that spooked them, had plunged down the gentle slope on either side. The panic went further than the eye could reach; to the south, it flooded toward the flat skyline of the prairie. To the north, in the bottom of the draw, it drove straight along the trail and the KP tracks for Railhead. There was a red glow in the sky over the town.

There was no chance to do anything about it; no chance to catch the leaders, even if he'd been able to ride hard. And one man couldn't turn them now. It would take an army.

Arn Hendricks did something then which he had not done within his memory before. He sat down and covered his eyes with his hands and wept.

It was daylight when he hoisted Luke Malette's body over the saddle horn and slowly rode toward town. Some of it was there, anyhow; in the clear morning air, he could see shapes against the skyline.

As he rode, he strained desperately to see details—movement in the street, the shape of a building—like a man who has been a long time away from home. The bank, the Methodist church, the parsonage beside it; these were simple enough. His eyes touched on the depot and then moved across the tracks, toward Joyville. The Paris Girl Saloon, distinguished by its peculiar humped roof, the Golden Horn—

He jerked the pony to a stop and .ose in the saddle. Joyville was still there. The tin and cardboard shanties, the canvas tents, the lean-tos—all the things that should have been obliterated as if by the swe .p of a broom. Every stick of it was still there.

He banged his heels into th , pony's ribs. The path of the cattle was easy to follow; the pounding hooves left a churned-up, mangled earth behind. He was still a quarter mile away when he saw where the swath broke off and swung to the south, as sharply as a prairie fire goes around a plowed fire-break. The break was less than a hundred feet ahead of the stock pens and the Exchange—or what was left of it.

There was still a handful of die-hards around the smoking remains of the building, some of them traders whose quarters had been there. He pulled up beside a bearded man in a derby hat.

"I still don't see— What happened?"

"She burned, brother!"

"I know that, but—"

"Somebody fired her, thank God Somebody with good sense. By the time those Texas critters got here, she was burning like the Unbelievers in hell, and it turned them. The flames was eighty feet high and it was better than a wall around the town. Lookahere, you can see where they—"

The words stuck in his throat. He goggled at the figure bent across the saddle horn.

"Wait a minute," he said. "Ain't that Luke Malette?"

"Yes," Arn said absent-mindedly. A wry smile lifted the corners of his mouth as he watched somebody pouring water over a strongbox in the ashes, trying to cool it enough to pull it out.

"Somebody fired her," he said. "Like you say—somebody with good sense."

THE REVEREND MR. MINNER FLATLY REFUSED TO BECOME the new mayor of Railhead, pointing out that his chief con-?ern was with things spiritual, not temporal. It was reputed that he also said that any man who had to serve in that par-:ular capacity was not only entitled, but required, to use .rofanity on occasion, and the Discipline expressly forbade this to men of the Methodist cloth.

He did consent, however, to act as temporary chairman at the first regular meeting of the city council after Doc Chubb's death. This was not quite two weeks after Arn

Hendricks brought Luke Malette home across his saddle horn, and it would have been difficult for a casual citizen to recognize the Council at all. Patterson, who ran the livery stable, and Arn Hendricks and the Reverend were the only familiar faces. Filling the other two chairs were Mr. Secundus Lawton, dealer in feed and hay, and Mr. Ralph Coleman, editor and publisher of the Railhead *Observer*. These gentlemen had been persuaded to act in a temporary capacity until a special election could be called to fill the gaps.

Mr. Coleman apparently regarded it as a very special occasion. Although he smelled strongly of peppermint, he was sober. This was in deference not only to the Acting Chairman, but to Miss Matilda Larson, who, when the regular business was concluded, had remarks.

"I've had a reply from this doctor in Kansas City," she told them, waving a letter. "He'd like to come, and he sounds all right. He's a young man, thirty-four. I think that's good for a young town."

Arn Hendricks cocked an eyebrow at her.

"I was very direct about the whole thing," Mattie said. "I told him exactly what our situation was here, informed him that the community was willing to provide him a house free of charge, and that there was an experienced assistant available."

"*Expert* experienced assistant," Reverend Minner said gallantly.

"And he does hold with the germ theory in medical practice."

"I don't like young doctors," Arn muttered. "Seems to me we want a more experienced man."

"Nonsense," Mattie said. "Get somebody to grow along with the town, the way Doc Chubb did."

Mr. Coleman heaved himself upright in his chair.

"In regard to the subject of growth," he said. "I learned something today that this august body ought to chew on. I got it straight from the Kansas Pacific railroad that nine major Texas shippers had canceled tentative arrangements for shipping space here. They're shifting to Dodge. The KP expects a lot more of the same."

"But this," Patterson said, "is the biggest cattle mart on the North American continent."

"You read that in my paper. It was therefore true—but." Mr. Coleman thumped the table with a meaty forefing "Dodge is just as close to the Red River, and the country oᴜ there isn't grown up yet. A herd moves faster on an open trail. And from what I hear of Dodge, it's cowboy heaven. The cattle trade in Railhead is going. Get it through your heads."

"It's a hard thing to believe." Minner shook his head.

"Not for smart people. The traders I talk to doubt if it's worth while to rebuild the Exchange. And the Soiled Doves, those true barometers of a community's moral tone, are migrating west like passenger pigeons—already. A smart man might conclude that this town is through."

He leaned back in gloomy triumph and blew peppermint at a June bug on his vest. There was a moment's silence.

"It had better not be," Arn Hendricks said quietly. "I've got thirty-three hundred dollars in credit on my books, and I owe twenty-eight hundred of it to somebody myself. The bluestem and the buffalo grass aren't moving to Dodge, are they? Winter wheat will still grow and a corn crop will make —at least sometimes—won't it?"

Mr. Coleman shrugged.

"I hope so. Before I moved, I'd have to pay my printer's back salary. I'm here for the rest of my life."

AT NINE O'CLOCK ARN WALKED MATTIE HOME, AND FOR A while there was little talk between them; Coleman's words still echoed in their heads.

"The cowhands gone; the fighting days over," Mattie said. "It's hard to think about."

"That all depends on your idea of a fight," Arn grunted. "I've got a business that has to pick up its feet and move. This town's got to buckle down and prove that it's an honest-to-God town, not a geographical accident. From here on, it looks to me as if the fight would get tougher."

He helped her across the street at the bank corner, and as they walked both of them turned, without thinking, and glanced toward he windows at the back. Hollow black squares against th lighter limestone.

"Arn," Mattie aid, "what have you got against the new doctor?"

"I told you; he too young. I like middle-aged doctors."

Her hand slid down his arm until the fingers touched his.

"Would it make any difference," she said, "if I told you that he said the house would have to be a big one, because there were three boys and one girl?"

Because it was dark here, he permitted himself the indis- tion of a full-fledged grin.

It might," he said.

While this conversation was going on, a rather stout man emerged from the stone building that served as jail, office for the marshal, and general catchall for city affairs. His name was O'Leary, and this was his second night on the job. Last night, when he started in, there had been a considerable

121

to-do, with prominent citizens in attendance and cheering in the streets. Tonight his glory was gone, and he was alone.

O'Leary wore no badge, and he carried no weapons. In his right hand he carried two poles about five feet in length. There was a small hook on the end of one of these. Secured to the end of the other was a piece of waste that had already been soaked in coal oil. Standing on the sidewalk, O'Leary struck a match on his shoe sole and lighted the waste.

He reached up and with the pole in his left hand unhooked the tiny window and swung it open. Then he reached up with the pole in his right hand and applied the flame to the wick. After a moment it caught, and a yellow glow fell on O'Leary.

And then he closed the tiny window and, with a pole under each arm, plodded down the walk to light the rest of the new lamps on the streets of the city of Railhead.